LITTLE LEAGUE
BASEBALL
WORLD
SERIES

MATT CHRISTOPHER

Ⓛ Ⓑ
Little, Brown and Company
New York Boston

Little, Brown and Company

Hachette Book Group
1290 Avenue of the Americas, New York, NY 10104
Visit us at lb-kids.com
mattchristopher.com

Little, Brown and Company is a division of Hachette Book Group, Inc.
The Little, Brown name and logo are trademarks of Hachette Book Group, Inc.

The publisher is not responsible for websites (or their content)
that are not owned by the publisher.

First Paperback Edition: January 2015
First published in hardcover in July 2014 by Little, Brown and Company

Matt Christopher® is a registered trademark of Matt Christopher Royalties, Inc.

Little League Baseball, Little League, the medallion and the keystone are
registered trademarks and service marks belonging exclusively to
Little League Baseball, Incorporated.

© 2014 Little League Baseball, Incorporated. All Rights Reserved.

Text written by Stephanie True Peters

Library of Congress Control Number: 2013043746

ISBN 978-0-316-22046-0 (hc)—ISBN 978-0-316-21295-3 (pb)

The Little League® Pledge

I trust in God

I love my country

And will respect its laws

I will play fair

And strive to win

But win or lose

I will always do my best

CHAPTER
ONE

Liam McGrath, twelve-year-old catcher for the Ravenna All-Stars of Southern California, shifted. His gaze flicked to the scoreboard beyond the left-field fence of Al Houghton Stadium. It was the bottom of the fifth inning of the West Regional Championship. The score was Guests 4, Home 7. Southern California was the visiting team.

His lips tightened. *We've got to get this guy out*, he thought. He returned his attention to the boy on the mound. *Time to turn up the heat, Phillip!*

Holding the baseball behind his back, pitcher Phillip DiMaggio leaned forward, narrowed his piercing black eyes, and glared at the Northern California batter. Liam wondered how the hitter felt being on the receiving end of that look. A little unnerved, he guessed. That's how he'd felt, anyway, whenever Phillip had turned that glare on him, back when they played on different teams during the regular Little League season.

If the Northern California player was bothered, though, he didn't show it. Nor did he seem troubled that there were two outs, that the count was oh-and-two, or that he could strand runners on first and second. Why should he? Earlier in the game, he had clocked a two-run RBI triple under the exact same circumstances. Only a spectacular throw from outfielder Rodney Driscoll to Liam had prevented that triple from turning into a three-run homer.

Ignoring the knot of anxiety in his stomach, Liam flashed the signal for a fastball. Phillip nodded once. Then he reared back, lunged forward, and threw.

Swish! Thud! "Strike three!"

The knot vanished. The batter stood stock-still for a moment and then retreated to the dugout. The scoring threat was over.

The Southern California boys hustled into the third-base dugout. Coach Driscoll rattled off the batting order.

"Phillip is up first. Matt, you're after Phillip. And then it's Rodney, Liam, and Mason. Quick bats out there, and even quicker feet when you get a hit." The coach smiled. "Right?"

"Sure thing, Dad," Rodney replied enthusiastically. Rodney was Coach Driscoll's adopted son. He had a brother, Sean, who was also adopted. Sean wasn't on the All-Star team, but he was in the stands, cheering for his brother and the other players.

Phillip stepped into the batter's box. He fouled off the first pitch for strike one. He straightened out the next one for a sizzling line drive past the pitcher and landed safely at first.

"Here we go, Matt, here we go!" Coach Driscoll called. The boys added their voices, quieted with the pitch, and then, leaping to their feet, bellowed with joy. Matt Finch slugged the ball far into the outfield for a stand-up double!

Runners on second and third, no outs. Excitement shot up Liam's spine as Rodney, one of the team's best hitters, approached the plate.

If Rodney gets a hit, I would be the go-ahead run. If I see a pitch I like...

He shook his head to keep his hopes from running away with him. He glanced at NoCal's pitcher—and those thoughts came racing back.

3

The boy on the mound had started the game. He had a good changeup and a great fastball. But neither pitch had stumped Liam. His first at bat, he'd hit a single. He got up again in the fourth and belted a double that earned SoCal its fourth run. Now the same pitcher had given up two straight hits.

When Rodney connected with the first pitch, Liam's heart started pounding. And when Phillip crossed the plate and Rodney landed safely at first with Matt staying put at second, Liam's heart threatened to burst right out of his chest.

As he adjusted his batting helmet, a hand dropped lightly onto his shoulder, startling him. "Deep breaths, son," Coach Driscoll murmured. "Deep, calming breaths."

Liam closed his eyes and inhaled slowly through his nose. He held the breath for a moment and blew it out slowly through his mouth. The breathing technique was something Coach Driscoll had taught him. A dentist by profession, the coach used it to soothe nervous patients. It worked just as well with nervous players.

Coach Driscoll handed him a bat. "Better?"

Liam grinned. "Much. Thanks, Coach." Buoyed by a wave of enthusiastic applause from his teammates, he left the dugout.

"Time!"

Liam froze at the umpire's call. He watched with dismay as NoCal's manager pulled his pitcher. When he saw who was coming in, his dismay turned to sinking dread.

Liam had faced the new NoCal pitcher once before in the West Regionals. Things had not gone well—not by a long shot.

Like his teammate, the boy had a good changeup and a decent fastball. He had a third pitch, too: a knuckleball that bobbled and danced its way through the air toward home plate. That was the pitch he'd thrown to Liam three times in a row.

And it was the one Liam had missed by a mile three times in a row.

There's nothing you can do about it, he thought ruefully, *so make the best of it.*

"Batter up!"

Liam squared his shoulders, strode to the plate, and hefted the bat into position. The pitcher wound up and threw. It was a knuckleball. Even though Liam had been expecting the pitch, he couldn't follow the ball's path. He let it go by, hoping it would miss the strike zone.

It didn't. The umpire made a fist for strike one. One pitch later, he repeated the gesture.

Sweat beaded on Liam's forehead. He wiped it away quickly and glanced at the mound.

The pitcher's lips twitched in a smirk.

And just like that, Liam's anxiety fled. Fierce determination took its place. He moved back into position with one goal in mind: to blast the ball out of the park and wipe that smirk off the pitcher's face.

The NoCal hurler leaned in, took the signal, reared back, and threw. Liam locked onto the ball the way a missile locks onto its target. He swung with all his might.

Pow!

CHAPTER
TWO

Carter Jones woke with a start. He blinked in the darkness, momentarily disoriented by his shadowy surroundings. Then he remembered where he was: the dormitory of the A. Bartlett Giamatti Little League Leadership Training Center in Bristol, Connecticut. He was in the top bunk of one of the beds. His friend Ash LaBrie slept in the bunk below. Other players from Forest Park, Pennsylvania, were in similar beds throughout the hall.

Carter rolled onto his side, wondering what had woken him. Suddenly, his head vibrated.

Bzzzz, bzzzz. Bzzzz, bzzzz.

He grinned, dug his hand beneath the pillow, and

retrieved the personal cell phone he'd stashed there earlier. Only Liam would be calling this late, and for only one reason: to tell him who'd won the West Regional Championship.

As quickly and quietly as he could, he slipped down the bunk bed ladder, speed-walked to the bathroom, and closed the door behind him. Then he answered the call.

"Doofus?" he whispered hopefully.

"Dork." Liam's voice was just as quiet.

No, not quiet. Subdued. As in, not the way it would sound if SoCal was the West Regional champ. Carter's heart sank.

Before Carter could think of something to say, Liam murmured, "I'm sending you a video clip. Watch it, then call me back." He hung up.

Carter blinked, not sure what to make of Liam's abruptness. His phone buzzed again, signaling that the video had been received.

He thumbed his way to the attachment, muted the volume, and hit play.

The video opened with a close-up of the Al Houghton Stadium scoreboard. According to the information there, it was the top of the sixth and final inning. The home team had seven runs while the guests had five. There were no outs, but the batter had a count of oh-and-two.

But which team is "Home"? Carter wondered.

He got his answer a moment later, when the shot pulled back to show the infield. Standing at first and second were runners in Ravenna uniforms, their cobalt-blue-and-white jerseys brilliant beneath the stadium lights. He tried to see whether Liam was one of the runners, but before he could, the image veered to home plate.

His eyes widened. Liam was the batter.

As Carter watched, Liam stepped out of the box and wiped his brow. The video zoomed in on Liam's face. He looked anxious.

Oh, no, Carter thought, biting his lower lip.

But a split second later, something fascinating happened. Liam's expression morphed from worry to fierce determination as he lifted the bat over his shoulder.

He's going to crush this next pitch! As the thought crossed Carter's mind, the Northern California pitcher hurled the ball toward the plate. Carter tried to see what kind of pitch it was, but the image on the screen was too small. Liam swung.

Pow!

Carter wished the video had followed the ball's

path. But it stayed on Liam, who dropped his bat and sprinted toward first, head down, legs churning, arms pumping.

"Go, Liam, go!" Carter whispered urgently.

Suddenly, Liam's head snapped up. A huge grin split his face. He leaped and punched the air with his fist. He touched first base and continued to second. But he wasn't sprinting anymore—he was practically galloping, each step filled with such glee that Carter didn't need sound to know what had happened.

Home run! SoCal was in the lead, 8–7!

Of course, NoCal had last bats, but the videographer—Carter guessed it was Liam's older sister, Melanie, who was making a movie about Ravenna's postseason—added a shot of the scoreboard at the end of the game. Guests 8, Home 7.

Ravenna had won the West Regional Championship! Next stop: the Little League Baseball World Series!

Impatient with excitement, Carter clumsily tapped the screen to back out of the video and contact Liam.

His cousin answered on the first ring.

"You doofus!" Carter hissed. "I thought—well, you *know* what I thought!"

Liam's laugh boomed in Carter's ear. Carter couldn't stop himself. He laughed out loud, too—and then clapped a hand over his mouth as the sound echoed off the bathroom walls.

"Gotcha good, didn't I?" Liam chortled.

"You rocketed that ball out of the park! What'd he throw you, anyway? A meatball?"

"Don't know, and right now, I don't care!" Liam replied. "What I do know is that I'll be seeing you in Williamsport!"

That assertion brought Carter up short. He *would* see Liam in Williamsport, true enough. But the question was, would he be there as a spectator, or would he and the other Forest Park All-Stars be among the sixteen teams in the World Series tournament?

He decided to look on the positive side. "I'll be there after we beat DC tomorrow—or today, I guess," he amended, knowing that it was well after midnight.

Liam chuckled. "Good thing your game isn't until late afternoon. You'll have plenty of time for a nap!" He gave a loud yawn. "Listen, I gotta get going. We're getting the bus to the airport really early. One last thing, though, dork"—Carter could hear the smile in his cousin's voice—"fist-bump, fist-bump, fist-bump."

Carter laughed again, this time not caring if someone heard him. Bumping fists three times in a row was his and Liam's way of wishing each other good luck.

He raised his left fist even though Liam couldn't see him. "Right back at you."

The cousins ended their call. Carter caught sight of himself in the mirror. He stared into his reflection's green eyes. He made a fist again and tapped it against the mirror.

"Good luck," he whispered. "And go get 'em."

CHAPTER
THREE

Psst!"

Liam jumped at the sound. He'd been so engrossed in his book, a sports novel by his favorite author, that he didn't hear the flight attendant approach.

Kate, according to her name tag, laid a finger on her lips and nodded toward his seatmate. Liam glanced over and suppressed a laugh. Phillip was out like a light, mouth open and head lolling on the pillow he'd propped up against the plane's small oval window.

"Where are we?" Liam whispered as he put down his book, unfolded his tray table, and accepted the bag of pretzels and soft drink Kate handed him.

"Somewhere over Ohio," Kate replied.

Liam yawned. He and his teammates had been traveling since early morning. A chartered bus had taken them; the Northwest champions from Obsidian, Wyoming; and the coaches for both teams from San Bernardino to the airport in Ontario, California, where they boarded a flight bound for Philadelphia. Another bus would take them to Williamsport.

Kate held out another bag of pretzels. "Would you like to save these for your teammate?" She grinned. "Or you can eat them if your friend doesn't wake up soon. I won't tell."

Liam took the snack and a second drink, too, and Kate moved to the next seats. As he munched a salty stick, he sneaked another glance at Phillip.

Your teammate, Kate had called him. *Your friend.* And yet just a few months ago, he wouldn't have been caught dead sitting next to Phillip.

He and Phillip had first met at last year's Little League Baseball World Series. Liam had been living in Pennsylvania and was a catcher on the Mid-Atlantic Regional championship team then. Phillip pitched for West. Their teams faced each other in the U.S. Championship. In the last inning, Liam came up to bat. Mid-Atlantic was down by a run, had two outs, and a runner

14

on third. Liam wanted to send that runner home something fierce.

Phillip was on the mound. His first pitch was a fastball. Liam thought it would miss the strike zone, but it didn't. Strike one. Liam nicked the second for a foul and strike two. When Phillip's next pitch came, Liam swung for the fences—and struck out to end the game, and Mid-Atlantic's chance to play for the World Series title. To make matters worse, the momentum from his powerful swing corkscrewed him off-balance. He'd landed face-first in the dirt—a humiliating moment caught on camera and later posted online for anyone to see.

In time, the memory of his colossal strikeout might have faded to nothingness. But a freak coincidence brought it back into crystal clear focus.

That winter, Liam's family moved from Pennsylvania to Southern California. To Phillip's hometown, to be exact. Liam didn't know Phillip lived there, though, until after Little League tryouts. To his relief, he and Phillip were assigned to different teams. They would meet on the field, but only a few times, not every practice and every game.

Knowing he'd face Phillip, Liam threw himself into the sport as never before. Phillip seemed to do the same.

Our unspoken rivalry made us both work harder, Liam thought as he finished his pretzels.

When they both made the All-Star team, Liam decided to clear the air. At the first practice, he marched up to Phillip and congratulated him on last year's World Series win. The bold move worked. Now here they were, winging their way across the country to play in that most celebrated youth sports event, the Little League Baseball World Series, not just as teammates, but as friends.

"Unbelievable," Liam murmured, "and awesome."

Phillip woke up with a snort. He stretched and pointed at the snacks. "Hey, are those for me?"

Soon afterward, a crowd of Northwest players gathered near their seats. The boys knew that Phillip and Liam had been to the World Series before. They peppered them with questions about their experiences.

"What's it like, playing in front of those huge crowds?" a sandy-haired boy wanted to know.

"I'm not going to lie to you," Liam answered. "When I ran into Lamade Stadium for my first game, I was a little intimidated. But then the game started, and everything else just kind of faded into the background, you know?"

The boy nodded. "Yeah, that happened to me this last tournament."

The conversation turned to the Dr. Creighton Hale International Grove. The Grove, as it was known, was where the players from all sixteen teams—eight from the United States, eight from regions around the world—lived during the World Series tournament.

"Here's how it works," Liam said. "You get a card that you keep with you at all times. That gets you into The Grove, so don't lose it or forget it!

"There are four dorms," he continued. "Each building is two stories tall. Four teams, two U.S. and two International, stay in each building—one U.S. and one International per floor."

"The recreation area is awesome," Phillip added. "Tons of stuff to do, like Ping-Pong, video games, television—"

"And a pool!" Liam cut in enthusiastically.

"What about the food?" someone called out.

"It's *so* good!" Phillip and Liam said in unison, drawing laughter.

One of the players wanted to know if he'd see his family at all.

"That is definitely an option," Liam replied. "You can arrange to go out to dinner or to the mall or the movies with them, meet up with them on days you don't have games, see them under this big tent—"

"And be sure to look for them at the Grand Slam Parade."

The Grand Slam Parade was a huge welcome celebration honoring all the Little League teams. Held in downtown Williamsport the night before the tournament began, it attracted thousands of fans. Liam remembered seeing his and Carter's families cheering and waving at them from the sidewalk.

"But, honestly, you'll be so busy with your other family," Phillip said, indicating the West and Northwest players, "you might not have much time to see them!"

The informal Q-and-A session ended soon after that. Many of the boys dozed off. Liam, however, thought about the parade.

Wonder if my family will be with Carter's this year, or if they'll hang out with other West parents.

He didn't know the answer, and after a while, he slept, too. He woke up when Kate shook him lightly.

"We'll be landing soon," she said.

Liam rubbed his eyes. "What time is it?"

"Almost six o'clock, East Coast time," she answered.

Liam sat up, instantly wide-awake. "Carter's game is about to begin!"

CHAPTER
FOUR

And starting on the mound for Pennsylvania in this year's Mid-Atlantic Regional final," the voice over the stadium loudspeaker boomed, "Ca-a-ar-ter Jones!"

Carter bounded out of the shade of the first-base dugout and onto the green grass of the baseball diamond. Whoops and cheers rose from the fans packed into the bleachers of Leon J. Breen Memorial Field. Carter slapped palms with the five boys already standing in line along the base path: second baseman Freddie Detweiler, first baseman Keith O'Donnell, right fielder Craig Ruckel, left fielder Charlie Murray, and catcher Ash LaBrie. Beneath their green-and-white caps, their faces shone with equal parts excitement, apprehension, and determination. Carter knew how they were feeling because he was feeling exactly the same way.

Carter took his place next to Ash. Ash nudged him and grinned.

"You ready?" the blond-haired, brown-eyed catcher asked, raising his voice so Carter could hear him over the crowd.

Carter returned his grin and nodded.

If people had told Carter eight months ago that he'd be playing in the Mid-Atlantic final, he would have said they were crazy. *Get that far in the postseason without Liam behind the plate? No way!*

Liam had been Carter's catcher from the time Carter began pitching in the Little League Major Division. But then Liam moved across the country.

Carter knew being uprooted was difficult for Liam. But it wasn't easy for him, either. Liam left a big hole in Carter's life, not to mention behind home plate. Carter hadn't expected anyone to fill either anytime soon.

Then Ash and his mother moved into the McGraths' house in January. Within a week, Ash was standing in Carter's living room, telling him he wanted to be his catcher that season. He stated his belief that if they teamed up, they could play their way to the World Series that summer.

Out of loyalty to Liam, Carter kept his distance from Ash at first. Then he and Ash were drafted onto the same Little League team, the Hawks. To his surprise, Carter found he worked well with Ash. Thanks in large part to their efforts, the Hawks took first place in their league. On June 15, both Carter and Ash were on the Forest Park All-Star roster.

Carter, Ash, and their new teammates meshed right from the start. They swept past the competition in the District tournament in June. Victory at Sectionals in mid-July advanced them to the State tournament, where they faced the best teams in Pennsylvania. They lost their first game at States, yet in the end they earned the right to represent Pennsylvania in the ten-day Mid-Atlantic Regional Tournament in Bristol, Connecticut.

Forest Park's winning ways continued in Bristol. On the first Saturday in August, they beat the team from the District of Columbia. The next day they defeated New York. Forest Park edged out Maryland on Tuesday and Delaware on Wednesday.

Going into the semifinal round on Friday, Pennsylvania was in first place with a record of four wins and no losses. There the team faced fourth-place Delaware for the second time. Six innings later, Pennsylvania had another check mark in the win column—and Delaware was out of the tournament. Earlier that day, third-place DC had surprised everyone by defeating second-place New Jersey. While Carter sympathized with the disappointed Jersey players, he was psyched to be facing DC, a team they had already beaten, in the championship.

He knew better than to get overconfident, however. Overconfidence could lead to laziness. Laziness could lead to errors. Errors could mean defeat—and defeat meant watching from the sidelines while the DC players packed their bags for South Williamsport, Pennsylvania, and the World Series tournament.

Am I ready? Carter thought as he slapped hands with shortstop Raj Turner, third baseman Allen Avery, center fielder Ron Davis, and substitutes Stephen Kline, Luke Armstrong, Peter Molina, and Charlie Santiago. *Am I ever!*

Last to jog through the introduction line were the coaches, Mr. Harrison, Mr. Filbert, and Mr. Walker. All three were beaming and looking every bit as excited as the players themselves.

The loudspeaker crackled. "We will now have a representative from each team come forward to recite the Little League pledge."

Charlie M., Forest Park's rep, joined a DC player at the microphone. "I trust in God. I love my country and will respect its laws," they said in unison. "I will play fair and strive to win, but win or lose, I will always do my best."

They stepped back into their lines. Coach Filbert and one of the DC coaches took their places to recite the Little League Parent and Volunteer pledge.

"I will teach all children to play fair and do their best. I will positively support all managers, coaches, and players. I will respect the decisions of the umpires. I will praise a good effort despite the outcome of the game."

Back in the dugout, the teammates listened intently as Coach Harrison delivered one final pep talk.

"What can I say that I haven't said already?" he asked. "You boys have impressed us with your talent, your drive, your team spirit, and your sportsmanship. Just keep doing what you've been doing, and you'll walk off that field as winners—whether you win the game or not. Now let's hear it!"

Carter and the others put their hands together and chanted, "Forest Park, one-two-three! Forest Park, one-two-three!" The chant ended when the boys flung their arms skyward with a triumphant yell.

Carter grabbed his glove and hustled out to the mound. He and his teammates took their last warm-ups, and then it was time to face the first DC batter.

Carter received the game ball from the home-plate umpire. The leadoff hitter approached the box. The fans stilled, their voices lowered to a respectful hush.

But they could have been screaming and stomping their feet for all Carter would have noticed. He leaned forward, the ball held loosely in his left hand behind his back, and waited for Ash to flash him the signal for the game's first pitch.

Yeah. He was ready.

CHAPTER FIVE

The doors of the bus closed with a wheeze and a thud, signaling the start of the last leg of the daylong journey.

"Just a few more hours," a boy from Northwest said excitedly as the motor roared to life, "and we'll be in Williamsport!"

"I wish we could transport there like they do in sci-fi movies," someone else commented. "I feel like I've been traveling forever."

A murmur of agreement rippled through the weary players. They'd been on the road, in airports, or above the clouds since breakfast. They'd crossed two time zones and lost three hours, for while it was four o'clock

Sunday afternoon in California, in Pennsylvania it was already seven Sunday evening.

Liam silently agreed that the trip had seemed endless. But unlike some, he was looking forward to the bus ride. He settled back into the thick padding of his seat and gazed out the tinted window as signs bearing the names of familiar Pennsylvania towns passed by.

"Man, I miss this place."

He hadn't realized he'd spoken out loud until Rodney, sitting next to him, said, "Would you move back if you could?"

Liam shrugged. "I don't know. Southern California is better than I thought it would be—"

"We Southern California natives thank you," Rodney deadpanned.

"—but I think Pennsylvania will always feel like home. No offense."

"None taken," Rodney replied. "Now, speaking of Pennsylvania..."

He stood up, pulled a slim, flat bag from the overhead compartment, and sat back down. "Ta-da!" With a dramatic flourish, he withdrew a computer tablet from the bag and switched it on.

"It's Dad's," he explained. "He said we could watch the rest of the Mid-Atlantic championship."

Two minutes later, the live game appeared on the screen.

"Wonders of modern technology," Rodney said with satisfaction.

Liam waited impatiently for the score to be shown. When it finally appeared, he gave a whoop. "Pennsylvania is up, 2–0!"

Phillip popped up from the seat behind them. "What inning is it?"

"Top of the fourth," Liam replied.

"Who's pitching?"

Liam hesitated before answering that question.

Phillip and Carter had a long-standing rivalry that stretched back to their first meeting at Little League Baseball Camp two summers before. That week, Phillip had played a prank on Carter that Carter hadn't found amusing at all. All might have been forgotten, however, if they hadn't met up again at last year's World Series tournament, where the rivalry had flared again.

Surprisingly, Phillip hadn't realized that Liam and Carter were cousins until this summer. When he did find out, he let Liam know—in no uncertain terms— that he didn't want Liam talking to Carter about him. Liam had agreed but let Phillip know—in no uncertain terms—that he would continue to talk to Carter about everything else. Phillip seemed to accept that, yet Liam still wasn't 100 percent sure Phillip wanted to hear the name "Carter Jones."

But if Mid-Atlantic wins the Regional Championship, Liam thought, *he's gonna hear me say that name a lot—and see me with him, too, because I'm going to spend as much time with Carter as I can!*

"Carter's on the mound," he said at last.

Phillip grunted and sat back down. A moment later, however, he asked Matt, who was sitting across the aisle from Rodney, to change places with him so he could watch the game, too. "If that's okay with you guys," he added with a glance at Rodney and Liam.

"I've got a better idea." Rodney called to three boys in the back of the bus, the only row that had five seats across, "Yo, Cole, Mason, Dom! Switch spots with us, okay?"

In the end, only Cole Dudley moved because Mason Sykes and Dominic Blackburn wanted to watch the game, too. They crowded on one side of Rodney, who held the tablet, and Phillip and Liam sat on the other.

"Everyone comfy?" Rodney asked.

"Shhh!" Phillip, Dom, and Mason hissed.

Liam didn't say anything. His focus was on the game—or, more specifically, on the pitcher's mound, where Carter now stood, waiting for the next DC batter to step into position.

The television camera slowly zoomed in on Carter's face.

"Southpaw Carter Jones has thrown a terrific game so far," the announcer informed viewers. "In four innings, he's given up just two hits."

"His fastball and changeup have proved challenging," a commentator added, "but it's that knuckleball of his that has really been confounding DC batters."

"It'd confound me, that's for sure," the announcer joked.

While the announcers were talking, the batter entered the box. Now the camera pulled back to show Carter going through his windup. With one fluid motion, he reared back, lunged forward, and threw. The ball sizzled right toward the catcher's mitt. The batter swung but missed by a mile.

Liam felt Phillip tense beside him.

"Dang," Mason said.

"You can say that again." Dom's voice was awed.

The boys watched in silence as Carter hurled two more strikes—and then, exhibiting the same precision and power, he threw another six, in ten pitches, to retire the side in order.

Mason looked at Liam. "Don't take this the wrong way, man, but I hope DC beats Pennsylvania because I'm not sure I want to face your cousin!"

Liam didn't comment because he wasn't sure what to say.

He'd seen Carter pitch a few games in the post-season. He knew his cousin was formidable on the mound. But what he'd just witnessed was better than anything he'd ever seen him do.

And yet, unlike Mason, he wasn't dreading facing Carter. Just the opposite, in fact. His heart thumped with excitement, his hands itched to hold a bat, and his mind burned with a competitive thirst only one thing could quench.

"Pennsylvania better beat DC," he said, "because I want a crack at him!"

CHAPTER
SIX

Somebody throw water on Carter," Charlie M. yelled as the Pennsylvania players entered the dugout, "because he's on *fire!*"

Carter grinned broadly.

"Well done, all of you," Coach Harrison said, beaming. "Carter, that brings you to fifty-five pitches. That's getting up there in the count, but if you're good for one more inning, I'd like to keep you in because DC's heavy hitters will bat in the top of the fifth."

"Absolutely!" Carter replied without hesitation.

The coach nodded and turned to talk to Peter, Pennsylvania's leadoff batter in the bottom of the fourth. Peter had come in for Ron at center field last inning, so this would be his first at bat. He looked nervous, but Carter knew that Coach Harrison could calm him down. Sure enough, by the time the umpire called for the first batter, Peter looked ready.

DC's pitcher was just as ready. He'd subbed in during the bottom of the third, after the starter had given up two hits and a walk to load the bases with no outs. Raj, the first batter the reliever had faced, had popped a high fly ball to right field. The ball was caught for out number one, but Charlie M. had tagged up and raced home, scoring Pennsylvania's second run. Both boys were all smiles when they returned to the dugout. Unfortunately, Allen, up after Raj, had grounded into a double play, ending Pennsylvania's chances of adding more to its side of the scoreboard that inning.

"Here you go, Peter, here you go!" Carter cried as the bottom of the fourth began. The other players were just as encouraging.

Peter looked the first pitch into the catcher's mitt, swung and missed the second, and ticked three foul balls before dribbling a grounder back to the mound. The pitcher fielded it cleanly and threw to first. Peter was out.

"Nice effort, good try," his teammates said when he returned, head down, to the dugout.

Stephen Kline, in for Freddie at second base, was up next. Before he stepped into the box, he tapped the fat end of the bat on the ground three times.

"Never seen him do that before," Charlie S. commented.

Stephen took a huge cut at the first pitch and— *pow!*—blasted it to deep left field!

"Never seen him do *that* before, either!" Charlie S. bellowed. "But I hope I see it again soon!"

The hit, good for a double, seemed to derail DC's defense. Luke Armstrong, in for Keith, reached first on an error. Craig was struck in the arm by an inside pitch that drew gasps from the fans, who applauded when he trotted, unfazed and unhurt, to first.

Bases loaded, one out, and now Charlie M. was at bat. The fastest boy on the team, he could usually be depended upon to reach base if he made contact. Unfortunately, he didn't get a chance to run because he went down swinging.

"Well, that smelled," he muttered, clearly disgusted with himself.

"Coulda been worse," said Allen.

"How?" Charlie demanded to know.

"Coulda hit into a double play like I did last inning."

Charlie stared at Allen's slumped shoulders and sat

down next to him. "Hey, we've all been there," he said, patting him awkwardly on the back. Allen looked up, gave a half smile, and knocked Charlie in the ribs with his elbow.

At the plate, Ash held the bat high over his right shoulder, twirling it in tight circles as he waited for the pitch. Carter leaned forward and started a slow clap.

"Ash. Ash. Ash. Ash," he murmured each time his palms met. His teammates joined the chant, pulsing out a steady beat with hands and voices. Then a new sound cut through their cries like a rifle shot.

Pow!

The boys leaped to their feet. "Go-go-go-go-go!" they screamed.

Jumping up and down and grabbing his nearest teammate for support, Carter willed the runners to fly over the base paths. They had nothing to lose after all. If the outfielder caught the ball, the inning was over. But if he missed it, Pennsylvania could score one, maybe even two runs!

The DC center fielder raced back, waving his teammates away. He stopped near the fence and raised his glove.

Carter held his breath. He tracked the ball as it

hurtled toward earth. The outfielder took a little side step, adjusted his glove, and waited.

It's going to land right in the pocket, Carter thought, his spirits sinking.

Instead, the ball struck the glove's edge and fell to the ground!

Stephen, already partway home, covered the rest of the distance in a flash to cross the plate standing up. While the outfielder scrambled to pick up the ball, Luke charged toward third.

"Keep going!" the third-base coach cried, windmilling his arm.

Luke touched the bag and motored for home. Behind him, Craig churned up the dirt between first and second and headed for third. And Ash hadn't slowed after tagging first.

The DC center fielder hurled the ball to his cutoff man. The throw was just short, and the ball landed in the grass. The cutoff man recovered it quickly, but by then Luke had thundered across the plate. Craig hit the dirt at the same time, riding the final few feet to third on his buttocks.

So the cutoff man threw to second. The second baseman caught the ball and whipped his glove around and down to tag Ash out.

Except Ash wasn't out, because the ball had fallen out of the second baseman's glove!

The umpire flung his arms out to either side. "Safe!"

The dugout erupted into ecstatic cheers. What might have been an inning-ending hit had instead yielded two runs and landed Craig in scoring position for a possible third!

But those two runs were all Pennsylvania added to its side of the board that inning. Carter, up after Ash, hit a bouncer right to the first baseman. The DC player barely had to move to touch the bag for the last out. Disappointed, Carter returned to the dugout.

Ash followed him in a second later and started to put on his catcher's gear.

"Great hit, man," Carter congratulated his friend.

To his surprise, Ash made a sour face. "I got lucky."

"Who cares?" Charlie M. said as he passed them on his way onto the field. "We got some runs and that's what counts! Sometimes half this game is luck!"

Ash and Carter hurried out of the dugout. "What counts for me," Ash said to Carter, "is earning a run because *I* did something right, not because *they* did something wrong. DC is a good team. The only way we're going to win today is if we're better."

"And the only way we're going to win the World Series," Carter added, "is if we play well as a team."

He and Ash stared at each other. Ash smiled. "I think we do."

Carter hesitated and then returned the smile. "You know what? I think we do, too."

CHAPTER
SEVEN

Look!" a Northwest player shouted. "Is that what I think it is?"

Liam and several other boys craned their necks to see through the bus's front windshield. It was night-time, and there hadn't been much to see for several miles. But the bus driver had just announced that they were approaching the Little League complex and now—

"That's Lamade!" Liam cried, pointing at a ball field illuminated by banks of brilliant white lights.

The players burst into applause and excited chatter. The Howard J. Lamade Stadium was the most famous Little League Baseball diamond in the world. Right next to it was Little League Volunteer Stadium, a smaller but no less impressive venue.

"I can't believe we're here," Cole said, his eyes round and his voice awed. Several boys near him murmured their agreement.

A few minutes later, the bus pulled into a parking area and coasted to a stop. The double doors opened with a sigh. An older man wearing glasses and a badge identifying him as one of the Little League hosts climbed aboard and called out, "Anyone here play baseball?"

Liam and the rest of the boys laughed.

"Well then," the man cried, his face crinkling with good humor, "you've come to the right place! Grab your stuff and come on out!"

While the players gathered their belongings, Liam hurried to the front of the bus. "Excuse me, sir," he asked the man. "But do you know who won the Mid-Atlantic championship? We were watching the game, but something happened to the connection and we missed the last inning."

"Our local boys from Pennsylvania, four to nothing."

Liam's face split into a huge grin. "A shutout! Way to go, Carter!"

The man gave him a curious look. "You know Carter Jones?"

"He's my cousin," Liam said proudly.

The man blinked and then smiled. "By gosh, you *are* the same Liam McGrath, aren't you? I didn't recognize you underneath all that hair! Bet you didn't recognize me, either." He took off his glasses, pulled a baseball cap out of his back pocket, and stuck it on his head. "How about now?"

Liam's eyes widened. "Mr. Matthews!"

Christopher Matthews had been one of Mid-Atlantic's team hosts during the World Series the year before. Each team was assigned two such volunteers, who spent the entire tournament with the players and coaching staff. The men and women—or "uncles" and "aunts" as they are called—shepherded the players around the facility, scheduled practice times, got them up for meals, and performed countless other tasks that ensured the team was well taken care of.

Liam and Carter had liked both of Mid-Atlantic's hosts—had liked all the Little League volunteers and staff, in fact—but they agreed that Mr. Matthews was their favorite. He was friendly and funny, and he had read more baseball books than any other person they'd ever met. He was kindhearted, too: When he saw Liam after the game-ending strikeout, he hadn't said a word. He'd simply wrapped him in a quick, tight hug.

"I can't believe I didn't recognize you right away," Liam apologized. "But I never saw you without your cap before. And since when do you wear glasses?"

"Since my wife caught me squinting at my book one time too many." Mr. Matthews put his glasses back on and waggled his eyebrows. "Make me look smart, though, don't they? Anyway," he continued, "looks like you're stuck with me again this year, since I'm one of the West hosts." He chuckled. "When I saw your name on my list, I thought, 'Naw, can't be the same kid.' But here you are! I'm sure there's a story behind you ending up in sunny California, which I want to hear later. But for now, tell me, how are you?"

"I'm really good, Mr. Matthews," Liam assured him. "Really."

"Excellent. Still..." Mr. Matthews studied Liam for a moment, then shook his head. "I can't imagine you and Carter playing on different teams. You were practically inseparable last year. What'll it be like for you this time around, I wonder."

"Different," Liam replied.

"Indeed." Mr. Matthews rubbed his hands together briskly. "Ready to see your dorm?"

"Can't wait!"

CHAPTER
EIGHT

Fffffff. Ffffffff. Ffffffff."

Coach Harrison was blowing up a huge inflatable globe. He pushed the plug in place, balanced the ball on his fingertips, and held it aloft for his players to see.

"We are on our way to the World Series," he said solemnly to the boys gathered next to the chartered bus that would take them from Bristol to South Williamsport. He silenced their cheers with a lift of his other hand. "On the ride to Pennsylvania, I want you all to think about where the other teams come from."

He spun the globe and pointed to a spot in the Southern Hemisphere. "Australia." He moved his finger up, across the equator. "Chinese Taipei." His finger shifted farther north. "Japan." He rotated the globe a half turn and tapped a spot in the Northern Hemisphere. "The Netherlands." A quarter turn more and his finger touched three spots near the equator and one far above it. "Venezuela, Curacao, Mexico, and Canada.

"Plus," he added, tracing a zigzag across the United States, "there are the seven other teams from the U.S.: Massachusetts, Florida, Michigan, South Dakota, Colorado, Wyoming, and Southern California. And then there's us."

He touched the state of Pennsylvania. "Forest Park is right about here. And South Williamsport is here." His finger didn't move.

"So here's what I want you to think about. Our families and fans can jump in their cars in the morning, drive to see us play, and then return to their homes at night. You can see them in person practically every day, even if it's just a wave and a shout." He twisted the globe back and forth. "How many fans from these other countries do you think will be here? Heck, how many from the U.S. are likely to make the trip?" He tossed the globe to Coach Filbert, who popped the plug and let out the air.

"My point is this," Coach Harrison continued. "Many of these players will be far away from their countries, their parents, everything that's familiar to them, for the first time in their lives. You won't be. You're not the hosts of the tournament, but you're the closest thing to a home team it has. So I ask you to reach out to players from other regions, other countries. Talk to them, trade pins with them, play video games with them."

Keith raised his hand. "But, Coach, what if they don't speak English?"

Coach Harrison smiled. "You all know the same language: baseball! Right?"

"Right!" the players shouted.

"Good. Now hop on the bus. We've got a tournament to get to!"

After the excitement of winning the Mid-Atlantic region, Carter was hoping for a quiet ride to South Williamsport. His hopes faded when Ash plopped into the seat next to him holding a three-ring binder.

Ash's favorite hobby was collecting facts and figures about different Little League teams. He read game results and recaps online, recorded pitching and batting stats, noted fielding errors and great plays, and listed team records.

Carter once had a page in that binder. Before they'd met, Ash had followed Carter's progress through the previous year's tournaments up through the U.S.

Championship. He'd shown Carter his page, using it as proof that Carter wasn't a good pitcher—he was a great one. That binder was gone, however, the pages ruined when Ash dropped it in a puddle. Now it seemed Ash had started a new one. Carter groaned when he saw it.

"It's not what you think," Ash said. "I thought you might like to see pictures of my dad."

Carter blinked. Until recently, he hadn't known anything about Ash's father—hadn't asked, to be honest, too afraid his questions might stir up some troubling emotions. As far as he knew, Mr. LaBrie wasn't in the family picture. He'd figured Ash's father had died or divorced Ash's mother, or maybe just left. The truth was, Mr. LaBrie was in the military and stationed away from home for months at a time. When Carter found out, he felt silly for having avoided the topic for so long.

Now he leaned forward eagerly. "Let's see."

Ash opened the binder. Beneath a plastic sleeve was a photo of a man who looked a lot like Ash. His blond hair was cut much shorter than Ash's, but it was the exact same shade. He had the same intense gaze as Ash, too. That gaze used to make Carter squirm when he was pitching and Ash was catching. But now he found it helped him focus.

45

The photo on the next page showed a younger Ash and his father on a beach, kneeling beside a series of channels dug in the sand. *Ash and Andrew and their massive sand construction!* the photo's caption read.

"That was taken a few years ago, when we lived near the beach in North Carolina," Ash said. "We spent all morning digging it, and then we ate lunch and watched as the tide came in and covered it."

"It's awesome," Carter said. He sneaked a look at Ash. "You miss him?"

Ash kept his eyes on the book. "Yeah. We thought he might be home by now, but..." He shrugged and turned to the next page.

They looked through the rest of the photos, and Ash explained where and when the pictures had been taken. Carter was amazed at how many different places his friend had lived. Only the last photos showed familiar locations and people. Shots taken during the Hawks' season filled several pages.

Carter laughed out loud when he saw one Hawk photo. He and Ash were sitting in a dugout with their arms around each other's shoulders. Their smiles were forced, as if the photographer had posed them and made them say "cheese."

What made the photo funny was the girl behind

them. She had jumped into the shot just as the picture was taken. Her long brown ponytail was in midswing. Her arms were raised high in the air, her Hawks jersey bunched up at her waist. Her eyes were crossed, and she had a huge, mischievous grin on her face.

Ash was cracking up at the photo, too. "Rachel," he said.

Rachel Warburton had been the lone girl on the Hawks roster. A good player with a great arm and an equally great sense of humor, she'd helped Carter stay loose during tense games with her lame jokes and silly antics. Still did, thanks to an illustrated book of jokes she'd made for him to take to tournaments. He carried it with him in his gear bag and peeked at the pages when he needed a good laugh.

"She'll be at the World Series, too, you know," Carter reminded him.

"For the Challenger Game. Yeah, I know," Ash said.

The Little League Challenger Division fielded teams of developmentally and physically challenged players. All Challenger players were paired with "buddies," boys and girls who helped them during games. Rachel was one of them. Her team was one of two chosen to play the annual exhibition game during the World Series.

"Think we'll see her?" Carter asked.

Ash snorted. "She's so loud, we're sure to hear her at least!"

Laughing again, they turned the page to find only blank sleeves.

"What goes in here?" Carter asked.

"Future photos, I guess," Ash answered. He grinned. "Like us holding the World Series champions banner!"

"Yeah!" Carter agreed enthusiastically. He flipped back through the binder, pausing now and then when a photo caught his eye. When he reached the first page, something dawned on him. Ash had moved around a lot. Did that mean he'd move again? And if so...when?

CHAPTER
NINE

Liam dove underwater and swam toward the shallow end of the pool. His lungs were nearly bursting when he surfaced. He flipped onto his back, breathed deeply, and stared up into the late-afternoon sky.

Monday had started bright and early with breakfast in the dining hall. The boys ate quickly, knowing that once they were done they'd get to visit the one place they'd all been longing to see: Howard J. Lamade Stadium. When they'd cleared their plates, Mr. Matthews led them out of The Grove. A few minutes later, they were all standing on a vast grassy slope overlooking the pristine baseball diamond.

"That's Lamade!" Christopher Frost said excitedly. "And we're standing on the Hill, aren't we?" He squatted down to pat the grass.

Mr. Matthews's face crinkled into a smile. "This is, indeed, the famous Hillside Terrace. It's empty now, but just you wait. First game, this entire area will be a sea of baseball fans sitting on blankets and beach chairs."

"And will kids really be sliding down the Hill on cardboard?" Christopher asked. "Like they're sledding on snow?"

Mr. Matthews laughed. "Likely so. That seems to be an unspoken tradition."

"I hope I get to try it," Christopher said wistfully. "I've never gone sledding before."

"You haven't?" Liam was shocked. Growing up in Pennsylvania, he had gone sledding practically every winter.

Christopher shrugged. "Not a lot of snow in Southern California. I've only seen it on the mountains. Can't really sled there, can you?"

Liam had no answer for that. But once again, he was reminded of how different California and Pennsylvania were.

After the boys took the grand tour of Lamade,

they visited Volunteer Stadium. Later, they had taken batting practice, eaten lunch, and been fitted for their uniforms. Then they'd been allowed to enjoy the rec room. Liam had kept an eye out for Carter the whole day but didn't see his cousin.

Tuesday morning started with a light practice. After that, the boys were told they could take a swim.

Liam dove under again and swam the rest of the way to the shallow end. He surfaced and held on to the side, his legs floating out behind him.

Suddenly, a hand grasped his ankle and pulled.

"Hey!" he cried, spinning around.

The hand released him. A moment later, a boy broke through the surface waves, his green eyes shining with mirth. "Gotcha, doofus!"

Liam's jaw dropped. "Dork!" he cried. He hurled himself at Carter, swamping them both in the chest-high water. They splashed and roughhoused until the lifeguard asked them to tone it down a little.

"When'd you get here?" Liam demanded to know as they floated next to each other.

"Yesterday after lunch," Carter said.

"How was your drive down from Bristol?"

"Long," Carter answered. "How about your trip from California?"

"Longer. So, any of the guys come to the pool with you?"

Liam kept his voice casual, hoping Carter wouldn't guess what he really wanted to know.

Carter wasn't fooled. "Don't worry. Ash is inside, in the rec room. That's where I'd be, too, except Coach Harrison heard your team was here at the pool. He gave me permission to come find you."

"He's such a great guy," Liam said, grinning partly because he was so happy to see Carter again and partly because he was relieved that he *wouldn't* be seeing Ash just yet. He caught Carter glancing around then, and gave a sly grin. "You don't have to worry, either. Phillip's grabbing a nap in the chair over there. If you stay quiet, maybe you won't wake him."

"I wasn't worried." But Carter's sheepish smile let Liam know he was relieved not to be facing his rival, either.

Liam floated on his back and stared at the blue sky. "Can you even believe we're back here?"

Carter slicked back the wet hair from his forehead. "I find it awesome and extremely weird at the same time."

"That is exactly what I think. And if my team ends up playing your team..." He left the sentence unfinished.

Neither boy said anything for a moment. Then Liam challenged, "So, wanna race?"

Carter slid him a sideways look. "Deep end and back, like last year?"

"Yep."

"I'll win again, like last year."

"Nope."

"I won every time, you know."

"That was then," Liam retorted. "This is now."

They asked a big-boned blond boy paddling nearby to start them and to judge who touched the wall first upon their return. A few other boys moved away to give them room. "I'll race winner!" one called.

"I'll take loser," another said.

"You are the loser," the first joked.

The boys all spoke with strong accents. "Where are you guys from?" Liam asked as he and Carter got into position.

"Oz," the starter said.

"Down Under," another added.

Carter and Liam exchanged confused looks. The starter and his friends burst out laughing. "Those are nicknames for Australia, mate. My name's Jon, Jon Burns. That's Jim, and the other bloke is Nigel."

"Nice to meet you, mate."

Liam and Carter introduced themselves. "Well, whenever you're ready," Liam said.

The Aussie held up a finger gun. "On your marks... get set... *go*!"

Carter and Liam shoved off, arms slicing the surface with steady strokes and legs thrashing violently behind. The waves turned choppy, making it hard for Liam to see Carter clearly. When he touched the deep-end edge and swung around, though, he realized with glee that he was ahead.

Liam ramped up his speed another notch, churning through the water with all his might. His arms screamed for him to ease up, his legs begged for rest, but he ignored their pleas until his fingertips brushed the pool's side. He whirled. Carter was there, too, panting for breath.

"Who won?" Liam demanded to know.

Jon showed Liam a tiny space between his thumb and forefinger. "You did, by that much."

Liam whooped.

"Go ahead and enjoy it," Carter said with a grin. "It's the only time you're going to beat me this tournament!"

For a while, the boys swam races with Jon, Jim, and Nigel. Then it was time to get ready for supper.

It was only later that night, when Liam was drowsing in bed, that Carter's words came back to him.

It's the only time you're going to beat me this tournament.

He knew Carter hadn't meant anything by it. But for some reason, that sentence had him tossing and turning for the next hour.

CHAPTER
TEN

Stop being such a coward, Carter rebuked himself. *Go talk to him!*

It was late Wednesday afternoon, and he and his teammates were making their way through the food line at the pre–Grand Slam Parade picnic. Hosted by a local university, the picnic was held outside under big white tents. One at a time, the teams filed past banquet tables loaded with food, the players filling their plates with hot dogs and hamburgers, salads and side dishes. They helped themselves to drinks and desserts, too, and found seats beneath another tent.

The West players were just approaching the food tent. They were easy to identify in their team jerseys and matching caps. Carter, moving through the food line with the other Mid-Atlantic players, picked out Liam right away. He also saw Rodney, whom he had met while visiting Liam earlier this summer.

Then he saw Phillip.

Last year, Phillip had taken him by surprise, popping out from a corner of The Grove rec room and calling him Number One Fan, the nickname he'd given Carter at baseball camp.

Carter hated that nickname. It made him feel stupid.

When he first met Phillip at camp, he'd been starstruck, believing Phillip was related to the late, great Joe DiMaggio. He'd asked Phillip to sign his camp jersey. Phillip had scrawled *To Carter Jones, DiMaggio's Number One Fan!* on the shoulder. Later, Carter remembered that Joe DiMaggio had no direct descendants, so there was no way he and Phillip were related. But the damage was done. Phillip had called him Number One Fan for the rest of camp.

This year, Carter intended to make the first move. Now that Phillip and Liam were teammates, friends even, it just made sense to put their past differences aside, he told himself. Off the field at least. On the field, well, that was another story.

In the past two days, he'd spotted Phillip twice in the dining hall and once at the pool. But he was always at a distance, so it had been easy to come up with excuses—he had to eat with his team, he wasn't going swimming anymore—to avoid crossing paths.

Now with the teams mingling at the picnic, a meeting seemed inevitable. Carter tried to psych himself up to approach Phillip. He wasn't having much luck.

I'll eat first, he decided as the Mid-Atlantic players found seats together, *then I'll go talk to him. I'll just walk up, stick out my hand, and say...something.* He figured that "something" would come to him. If it didn't, the handshake would be a start. *One step at a time.*

When he stood up to dispose of his trash fifteen minutes later, his stomach still flip-flopped with nerves. *Here goes nothing,* he thought.

Rodney Driscoll suddenly appeared in front of him.

"Dude!" Rodney cried. "I was hoping to run into you here!"

"Hey, Rodney!" Carter said, grinning. "It's awesome to see you! But I can't hang out right now. I'm going to—"

"—talk to Phillip?" Rodney interrupted with a knowing glance from Carter to Phillip and back. When Carter nodded, Rodney pulled out his phone. "Before you do, don't you want to hear what he's been saying about you?"

The smile slipped from Carter's face. "Hang on. DiMaggio's been talking about me?"

"Mmm-hmm. Look at this." Rodney swiped his finger across the phone's surface and held it out so they could both see the screen. "Your cousin Melanie sent this video clip to me."

As part of her documentary about Ravenna's tournament experience, Melanie had interviewed many of the players, their families, and their coaches. The video on Rodney's phone was a joint interview with Liam and Phillip. Rodney thumbed up the volume so they could hear over the picnickers.

"Liam and I got off to a rocky start back at the Little League Baseball World Series," Phillip was saying. "I'm not going to go into what happened there, though, because it's all in the past."

Rodney fast-forwarded. "That's not the interesting part. Here we go." He restarted the clip.

"And what about Carter Jones?" Melanie asked from offscreen. "Is he in the past now, too?"

On-screen, Liam's eyes narrowed. His lips tightened.

Carter sucked in his breath. He could read every one of Liam's expressions. That look was a warning to

Melanie to back off. He could think of only one reason for that warning. *Liam's worried about what Phillip might say about me.* That made Carter worried, too.

Phillip shifted slightly in his seat before replying. "Carter and I have had some issues," he acknowledged.

Carter braced himself for Phillip's interpretation of their "issues."

"But I respect him," Phillip said.

Carter's jaw dropped. Next to him, Rodney started laughing.

"He's a really good pitcher," Phillip continued. "He'd have to be, I guess, to learn how to throw a knuckle-ball. I mean, I couldn't do it."

Liam's expression changed to one of astonishment. "Wait, you tried to learn the knuckleball?"

Phillip nodded. "Tried. Failed. Gave up, actually."

Liam's laugh boomed out of the phone's tiny speakers. "Good thing, considering I'm your catcher now. See, I tried to catch Carter's knuckleball. Tried. Failed. Gave up, actually."

Rodney hit the Stop button then. "Did you hear the key phrases?" he asked mischievously. " 'In the past. I respect him. Really good pitcher.' " He waved the phone. "I can replay the clip if you missed them!"

Carter jabbed him in the ribs. "Very funny!"

"Oh, there's one other thing, too," Rodney added. "I don't have it on video or anything, so you'll have to take my word for it. Before the West Regional Tournament, Phillip told Liam he never should have played that prank on you at baseball camp."

Carter stared at Rodney. "You know about that?"

Rodney nodded. "Phillip mentioned it once. I asked Liam about it later, and he told me."

"Oh. So you know there's been some bad blood between me and Phillip since then." Carter jerked his chin at Rodney's phone. "What I don't get is why you shared that with me."

Rodney smiled. "I'm a big believer in fresh starts, Carter. Sean and I got one years ago, when our dad adopted us. We hoped Liam could have one in California, which is why we never brought up his World Series strikeout." He gestured to the players around them. "This tournament should be about baseball, about playing with and against people from all over the world who love the sport the way we do. I didn't want an old grudge to ruin that for you or Phillip—or to get in the way of you playing the best ball you can. *That's* why I showed you the clip."

Carter nodded slowly as Rodney's words sank in. Then he looked over to where Phillip was sitting.

At that same instant, Phillip glanced up. He and Carter locked eyes.

A year ago, Phillip's gaze would have been mocking and loaded with smugness. The connection would have sent a jolt of anxiety through Carter's system. But this year, Carter saw something different in Phillip's eyes.

It's like he's hoping I'll come over, Carter thought with a start.

But before he could make a move in that direction, one of his team hosts hurried over to him. "Sorry to interrupt your conversation, Carter, but it's time to board the shuttle bus for the parade. You should probably join your team, too," she said with a nod to Rodney.

"Will do!" Rodney turned to leave.

Carter caught him by the arm. "Thanks, man."

Rodney's smile was full of warmth. "Happy to help."

CHAPTER
ELEVEN

"And how did Carter seem after you shared that clip with him?" Liam asked curiously.

Rodney had told him about his conversation with Carter on the ride over to the parade. Now they were climbing onto their float, one of eight decorated with the Little League World Series team colors and names, each carrying one U.S. and one International team.

But the parade was much bigger than those eight floats. Other flatbed trucks were decorated by area businesses and attractions. One carried a musical group with a singer, a drummer, and two guitar players. Local dignitaries rode in fancy cars while people in costume or uniform lined up behind banners bearing their groups' names. Marching bands and baton twirlers added to the festive mood.

"Seemed happy and relieved," Rodney replied to Liam's question. "I think he'd have gone over and talked to Phillip right then if we hadn't had to get on the buses."

"That's really great," Liam said. "They'll both have a better time here if they're not always looking over their shoulders."

Rodney slid him a look loaded with meaning. "Know anyone else who might benefit by making peace with a rival?"

Liam kicked the side of the float. He knew what Rodney was suggesting: He should let go of his jealousy and resentment of Ash once and for all. As he looked around at the excited players and paraders, he realized his friend was right.

If I keep hanging on to those bad feelings, he thought, *then I won't really be able to enjoy this tournament. So I've got to ditch them.*

Suddenly, he wanted to find Ash right away. It was impossible, though. He couldn't leave the float. Then he spotted a man in a Mid-Atlantic jersey pushing his way through the throng. Liam jostled his way to the side of the truck bed and yelled, "Coach Harrison!"

For a second he thought his former Pennsylvania

coach hadn't heard him. But then Coach Harrison stopped and looked around. Liam waved frantically.

The coach grinned. "Liam!" he called. "Long time no see! Huge congratulations on winning your Region!"

"Thanks, Coach. You too! Listen, can you—"

"I'm sorry, Liam, but I can't talk right now," Coach Harrison interrupted. He held up a Mid-Atlantic baseball cap. "Craig forgot this on the shuttle bus. We'll catch up later, okay?" He turned away.

"No! Wait! Coach! Can you give Ash a message from me?"

The coach gave Liam a surprised look. "Ash? Not Carter or one of your old teammates?"

"Ash," Liam said firmly. "Please tell him…" He searched for the right words. "Tell him I said congratulations on winning the Region and that I hope we can get to know each other this week. And that I think—no, I *know*—that Carter's in good hands with him behind the plate."

Coach Harrison's grin broadened. "I'll tell him. Have fun tonight!"

"You too!" Liam waved good-bye. He felt as if a weight had been lifted off his shoulders.

"You heard the man," Rodney said, bumping his shoulder into Liam. "Let's have fun!"

Phillip joined Rodney and Liam. He handed each boy a sack of wrapped candy. "We're supposed to toss this candy to the kids during the parade."

Rodney peeked inside his bag. "Good thing Sean isn't here. Half of this would be gone before the parade even started!"

Sean had never been bothered that he hadn't made the All-Star team—until he learned that he couldn't travel with his brother and father to the tournaments. During Regionals, he'd stayed with relatives who lived near San Bernardino. But they had no family in Pennsylvania.

"Can't I stow away in the cargo hold?" he'd begged his father on their last morning in San Bernardino. "Just put me in a dog crate. I'll be fine!"

"And where would you stay when you got there?" Coach Driscoll had asked.

"You'll rent me a hotel room?" Sean had replied hopefully.

But the coach's answer had been a firm no. Rodney and Coach Driscoll had boarded the bus for the airport, and Sean had gone back to stay with his relatives.

The boys' conversation was interrupted by a booming voice announcing the start of the Grand Slam Parade. Adrenaline shot through Liam's veins. He gave a whoop. As he did, he caught the eye of a player from the Netherlands, the International team that shared the West's float. They'd never met before, but that didn't matter. They grinned at each other in mutual glee as the procession left the staging area and rounded the corner to Millionaires' Row, the historic main street that cut through downtown Williamsport.

Roars and cheers from thousands of spectators lining the street greeted the participants as they came into view. Liam felt enveloped by the sound—and he loved it.

"This...is...*awesome!*" Rodney bellowed, underhanding a fistful of candy to a group of shouting kids.

One of the kids shouted louder than the others. He jumped up and down, too. "Hey! Hey! Rodney! Surprise!"

Rodney's jaw dropped when he saw who it was. "Sean?! How—when—*huh?*"

"Surprise!" repeated a deep voice full of laughter behind the boys. It was Coach Driscoll. He was grinning from ear to ear.

Rodney stared at him, dumbstruck.

"I didn't want him to miss this," the coach said. "He came with the McGraths."

"Is he staying with the Joneses, too?" Liam asked. His sister and parents were sleeping at Carter's house, a short drive from Williamsport.

"Actually," Coach Driscoll said, "the Joneses were

kind enough to arrange for Sean and your family to stay at the LaBries'. Apparently, Mrs. LaBrie is staying with a friend in Williamsport during the tournament, so her house was going to sit empty."

It took Liam a moment to process what the coach just told him. "Wait a minute," he said slowly. "Are you telling me that Sean is staying in my old house?"

CHAPTER TWELVE

The weather during the parade had been picture-perfect, but on Thursday morning, Carter woke to see gray clouds scudding across the sky. By nine thirty, the clouds had darkened to an angry black.

"Think the opening ceremonies will get rained out?" Charlie S. asked Carter as they dressed in their Mid-Atlantic uniforms.

Carter hoped not. He liked the pageantry of those ceremonies almost as much as the Grand Slam Parade.

The parade had been a blast. The streets had been packed with fans. Though the signs and banners in support of the "home" team from the Mid-Atlantic Region outnumbered those for the other regions, the cheers and applause had been for all the players. The best moment for him, however, was seeing the astonished look on Ash's face when Coach Harrison delivered Liam's message.

"Do you think he really meant what he said?" Ash asked Carter later.

"Absolutely," Carter assured him.

Ash chewed his lip. "Do you think I should stop worrying about him and focus on playing awesome baseball?"

Carter laughed. "Absolutely!"

"Then that's what I'll do."

"Me too," Carter said.

Miraculously, the storm held off, and the opening ceremonies started at eleven o'clock as planned. First up was Dugout, the Little League mascot, who led flag bearers around the infield of Volunteer Stadium. Then, as the song "It's a Small World" piped out of the loudspeakers, all the teams marched onto the field behind their banners, the players waving their caps at the crowd. The umpires joined the teams on the field, too.

After that, the mayor of South Williamsport gave a short speech. The mayor of Williamsport followed with a speech of her own. The Little League president and finally the league's chairman of the board also spoke. All congratulated the players on their achievements, thanked the parents and volunteers for their support and tireless efforts, and offered their hopes for a competitive yet fun-filled tournament.

They also talked about the opportunities for the players to make new friends. "We are proud and honored to welcome people from all over the world to this baseball haven," the chairman said as he gestured to the fields and buildings nestled snugly at the foot of a mountain. "In the days ahead, the players from our sixteen teams will have the chance to learn about the different cultures represented here today." He smiled. "And if previous tournaments are any indication, one of the top questions will be 'What's your favorite food?'"

Laughter rippled throughout the stands and the players and officials on the field.

"A second question often is 'Who is your favorite player?'" the chairman went on. "After recitation of the player and Parent and Volunteer pledges, it will be my pleasure to introduce you to one of mine."

Most of the pledges were given in English, but others were in the teams' native languages. As Carter listened to Kita Hiro from Japan, he was struck by how different Japanese was from English—and impressed when he overheard the boy speaking English to one of his team hosts later.

If I get the chance, I'm going to ask him to teach me some Japanese phrases, he decided.

His thoughts were interrupted then by a final announcement from the chairman. "Ladies and gentlemen, please give a warm welcome to one of my favorite players—Nathan Daly!"

Carter applauded wildly as an athletic-looking man trotted to the mound. Nathan Daly was a legendary professional pitcher. He'd been at the top of his game four years ago, his incredible fastball serving up more strikes than any other hurler at the time. His image had graced the covers of several sports magazines, the arresting stare of his grass-green eyes and his nearly white blond hair making him instantly recognizable.

Then two seasons ago, he stunned the baseball world by announcing his retirement. Fans had been up in arms—until they learned the reason why.

Daly's young wife had cancer and wasn't expected to live. Nathan Daly chose to be with her during the time she had left. It wasn't long. Six months after she was diagnosed, she passed away with Nathan by her side.

Daly kept out of the spotlight for a while after that. Recently, though, he'd put his glove back on and taken to the mound again—not as a professional player, but to help raise funds for cancer research.

"I can't believe he's here," Carter said excitedly to Ash. "He started his career in Little League, you know, just like us!" He watched as Daly went through his windup and threw to the catcher. "Man, what I wouldn't give to pitch like him."

Ash nudged him with his shoulder. "Dude, you keep throwing the way you do, and someday you will." He nodded as if the truth of this statement was evident. "You will."

"I'd be happy just to meet him."

As the words were leaving his mouth, Carter glanced at the West players. There he saw a sight he'd never seen before: Phillip DiMaggio staring in openmouthed adoration.

In the past, Carter had seen Phillip look smug, had watched him swagger with self-satisfaction, had endured his arrogant comments. But see him follow someone with worshipful eyes? Never!

"Guess he'd like to meet him, too," he murmured.

"What'd you say?" Ash asked.

"Nothing," Carter replied. "Just thinking out loud."

The ceremonies concluded. All but two teams made their way to the Grove dining hall for lunch. Mexico and Canada were scheduled to play the tournament's first game at one o'clock at Volunteer Stadium.

As Carter passed the nervous players, he gave them a big smile and a thumbs-up. "Good luck!"

"*¡Sí!*" Charlie S. echoed in Spanish, "*¡Buena suerte!*"

A few of the Mexican players nodded at Charlie S. with appreciation. "*¡Muchas gracias!*" one called back.

Charlie S. waved his hand. "*¡De nada!*"

Carter stared at his teammate. "Since when do you know Spanish?"

Charlie blushed. "My grandmother has been teaching me since I was little. I promised her I'd use it here if I could."

Just then the team from Japan made its way past them, the players chatting excitedly in their native tongue. Charlie S. and Carter smiled and waved to them, and they returned the gesture with slight bows and wide grins.

"Guess you don't always need to speak the same language to get the message across," Charlie S. commented.

"But we *do* speak the same language, remember?" Carter spread his arms wide as if to embrace their surroundings. "Baseball!"

CHAPTER
THIRTEEN

I wish we weren't facing the guys from Northwest," Rodney said as he pulled on his jersey. It was Friday afternoon, and West was scheduled to play its first game in two hours. "I mean, we're friends now because of Regionals and the trip here. It's going to stink if we beat them, you know?"

"Not as much as if we lose to them," Phillip interjected.

"Well, yeah, obviously," Rodney said, rolling his eyes.

Liam said nothing. With the time before their game ticking down, his nerves were beginning to jangle. He knew he'd be fine once he hit the field, but the anticipation was driving him nuts!

Finally, Mr. Matthews came to fetch them. "You boys will be playing to a packed stadium today," he informed them with a smile. "But don't you worry about that. These are some of the best fans in the world. No matter how you play, they'll cheer for you."

"Big crowds don't bother us, do they, guys?" Phillip said. He stretched his arms out to either side. The rest of the players imitated his pose. They waved their arms up and down with undulating movements and waggled their hips. "Loosey-goosey! Loosey-goosey!" they cried.

Phillip had introduced the crazy move during Regionals. Its silliness made them forget their nerves, at least temporarily.

Mr. Matthews laughed. "Reminds me of how I used to dance back in the old days. In all seriousness, boys, let me give you one suggestion. Use your warm-up time to work out any last jitters. Then block out the crowd and"—he grinned—"have a ball!"

Liam, for one, took the host's advice to heart. By game time, he felt raring to play. Not that he'd be playing right away. Coach Driscoll had chosen to keep him, Phillip, Cole, and Carmen on the bench for the first few innings. Liam was a little disappointed not to start, but he trusted the coach's judgment. After all, it had gotten them this far.

Northwest had won the coin toss and so was the home team. As the players ran onto the field, the West team and coaches huddled in a circle, arms over shoulders. They bounced on the balls of their feet and started murmuring.

"We believe. We believe. We believe that we can win."

The chant started low but swelled until it echoed throughout the dugout. "We believe! We believe! We believe that we can win!"

As Liam looked around at his teammates' excited and eager faces, he truly did believe it.

The first inning saw textbook baseball defense in action with both sides going three up, three down.

West's bats talked louder the second inning, however. Rodney started things off with a smashing double that had fans roaring with approval. Christopher followed up with a powerful single to the outfield. Rodney hotfooted it to third and then raced home for the first run of the game. Christopher stayed put at first.

Next up was Mason. He took a big cut at the first pitch and missed. He fanned at the next two pitches as well for out number one.

Nate Solis, a quiet twelve-year-old with thick dark eyebrows, brown eyes, high cheekbones, and full lips, fared better: getting to first when the Northwest shortstop missed his hard-hit grounder. Christopher slid safely into second, just beating out the throw after the bobbled pickup.

Luis Cervantes approached the batter's box with one out and runners on first and second.

Ping!

He drilled a line drive into the gap in shallow right field. He dropped his bat and dashed for first. Christopher and Nate took off, their legs blurring as they ran. Christopher scored and Nate landed safely at second. Luis was all smiles at first, clearly delighted to have clocked an RBI. "Keep it going, Elton!" he cried.

Unfortunately, Elton Sears ended their chances of adding a third run that inning by hitting into a double play.

"Rats!" Elton berated himself in the dugout.

"Shake it off," Coach Driscoll advised, "and focus on the inning ahead."

But Elton couldn't seem to shake it off. He walked the first two batters. Luis called for time and hurried to the mound. He said a few words to Elton and trundled back to the plate. Whatever he said must have helped because Elton threw two strikes.

On the third pitch, though—*pow!* The Northwest

batter connected for a high fly ball to shallow right field. Rodney tore up the turf trying to get to it.

Liam leaped off the bench. "Go, Rodney! Go!" he screamed. Then his heart sank.

He's not going to get there in time.

The Northwest base coaches weren't counting on Rodney to miss, however. They motioned for their runners to pause halfway down the paths. That way, if Rodney did make the catch, they could hustle back to their bases. But the lead runner must have missed the signal because he didn't put on the brakes until he was close to third.

Rodney, meanwhile, dove forward, slid on his side with his glove outstretched, and caught the ball! A split second later, he was back on his feet and throwing to second. The Northwest runner tried to backtrack, but he was too late. The ball hit Christopher's glove and stuck there.

"Out!" the umpire called.

"Way to go, Rodney!" Liam yelled. He high-fived Phillip.

But the scoring threat wasn't over yet. The next batter singled, putting runners on first and second. Then the one after that struck out to end the inning.

West 2, Northwest 0.

West widened the gap in the third thanks to more solid hits. Dom got on with a single. James Thrasher hit Dom to second but was thrown out at first. Matt knocked in Dom with an RBI double. Rodney walked, but Christopher flied out. Mason hit an impressive line drive, which had both Matt and Rodney crossing home plate. Then Nate struck out to end West's rally.

Northwest managed to put one run on the board in the bottom of the inning, but that was all.

West 5, Northwest 1.

Both teams made substitutions in the top of the fourth. Northwest put a new pitcher on the mound. Although he walked Cole, in for Luis, he struck out Carmen, who had taken Elton's place on the mound.

Then Dom singled, sending Cole all the way to third. Phillip was up next, having come in for James. After six pitches, he drew a walk.

Bases loaded, one out.

Matt popped a foul ball behind home plate. The catcher leaped to his feet, tearing off his mask. He twisted around and made the catch. Even though Liam was disappointed for Matt, he had to admire the catcher's heads-up play.

Bases loaded, two outs.

"Run on anything!" Coach Driscoll yelled, clapping as Rodney approached the batter's box.

Rodney watched the first pitch go by for strike one. He swung at the second.

Ping! It was a long ball in the air, heading for deep left field!

"It's a homer! It's a homer!" Liam cried excitedly.

The runners barreled around the bases—only to slow to a stop when the Northwest outfielder made the catch.

WEST 5, NORTHWEST 1, the scoreboard read when Northwest came up to bat in the bottom of the fourth— and that's how it stayed thanks to superb pitching from Carmen.

Liam, in for Christopher, congratulated the hurler in the dugout. Then he put on a batting helmet and selected a bat.

"You got this, Liam," Dom shouted, a cry picked up by the other boys.

As Liam strode to the plate, he glanced at the pitcher, a pleasant boy he had enjoyed chatting with on the plane ride from California. He wasn't thinking about that when he got into his stance, though. The only thing on his mind was getting a hit.

The first pitch came zipping in. Liam liked the looks of it. He swung.

Ping! His bat connected with the ball for a sizzling grounder toward third. Liam sped to first—and beat the throw!

Mason got a hit, too, but unfortunately, his wasn't as strong. To make matters worse, he stumbled a little as he started toward first. The shortstop scooped up the ball and threw Liam out at second. The second baseman relayed to first, catching Mason a few steps shy of the bag. When Nate struck out, the inning was over.

"Rats!" Mason said in the dugout. "I can't believe I tripped. That was totally embarrassing."

"Hey, don't sweat it, man," Liam said. "We've all done it!"

"Yeah, but not in the World Series." Mason hurried, head down, onto the field.

"Whoa, whoa, whoa!" Liam caught up to him. "First of all, everyone makes outs. Second of all, stop thinking about this as the World Series! Think about it like it's just another game. Okay?"

Mason looked up. He gave a small smile and then nodded. "Okay. Thanks, Liam."

"You bet! Now let's win this game!"

Northwest didn't score in the bottom of the fifth. West didn't add runs their last turn up, either. In the bottom of the sixth and with the game on the line,

Northwest put a run over to make it West 5, Northwest 2. They came close to posting another with a high fly to the outfield. Matt called for it, raced the short distance to get under it, and—

"Yes!" Liam murmured under his breath when Matt slapped his hand over the ball in his glove for the final out. "We did it—and we'll do it again! And we will go all the way!"

CHAPTER
FOURTEEN

Three hours after West's victory, Mid-Atlantic took to the field for its game against Midwest. The Midwesterners hailed from a small town in South Dakota called Triumph, a fact that had spawned such headlines as TRIUMPH TRIUMPHANT IN REGIONALS!, OTHER TEAMS "TRI" BUT LACK "UMPH"!, and the most recent one: WILL TRIUMPH TRIUMPH AT WORLD SERIES?

"Only time will tell," Ash had declared with a snort when he saw the headline.

The game started at eight o'clock Friday night. A full moon shone above Lamade, its silvery face like a beacon in the darkening sky. Below, the brilliant stadium lights illuminated the bright green grass, white lines, and red-brown base paths of the field. The muggy August weather was a little cooler than it had been when the sun was out, but not by much. By the time warm-ups were through, the players' hair and jerseys were damp with sweat.

Coach Filbert pointed the boys to a watercooler when they returned to the dugout. "Drink up, drink up."

Carter grabbed a cup of water. He wasn't starting, but he listened as Coach Harrison went through the lineup one last time: Stephen at second base, Keith at first. Craig in right field, Ash in center field, Charlie M. in left. Allen was at third and Raj was at shortstop. Luke was on the mound with Ron catching. That was the batting order, too, at least for the first innings. Carter knew it would change a bit when he and the other substitutes got in.

That time came at the top of the fourth. Mid-Atlantic was up, 3–1. The score might have looked a little different, however, if not for a few well-executed plays by the Pennsylvania team in the first half of the game.

In the bottom of the second, Midwest had had runners on first and second. There were two outs. The next batter knocked a grounder that bounced past Raj Turner. Charlie M. raced in from left field, scooped up the ball, and made a pinpoint throw to Allen Avery to nail the lead runner at third. The scoring threat was erased, and the inning was over.

Raj gave a great defensive effort himself in the third inning. This time, Midwest had a runner at second with no outs. The batter socked a sizzling drive back to the mound. Luke stuck out his glove but clipped the ball instead of catching it. Quick as a cat, Raj darted forward and snared the ball before it hit the ground. He whirled around, prepared to throw if the runner had moved off the bag. The runner wisely stayed put, only to see his chances of reaching home vanish when the next two batters struck out.

Unfortunately, Mid-Atlantic didn't add any runs in the top of the fourth.

"Stop 'em!" Ash hollered from the dugout as Charlie S. replaced him in center field. Peter trotted to the mound to take Luke's place, while Freddie hurried to second to take over for Stephen. Carter gave Ash a thumbs-up and headed to the hot corner, where he was subbing for Allen.

The first Midwest batter strode to the plate. A burly boy with a broad, round face and deep-set eyes, he hit a short grounder just inside the first-base line. Keith must have thought it was going foul, because he hesitated before lunging toward it. He was too late. The runner made it safely to first despite a quick pickup and throw from right fielder Craig.

The next batter hit a dribbler toward first. He was thrown out, but the runner reached second. The third Midwest hitter grounded to Raj. Raj checked the runner at second and then threw to first. But the batter reached the bag a split second before the ball. There were runners on first and second and still one out.

Carter shifted from foot to foot and bounced on his toes. His heart drummed out a fast beat. *Stop 'em! Stop 'em! Stop 'em!* it seemed to repeat.

Ping!

The fourth batter sent a short pop fly arcing just out of Raj's reach. Luckily, Ash swooped in and nabbed the ball before it hit the ground.

"Out!" the umpire cried.

The next hitter pinged the ball knee-high toward third base. Carter moved to meet it. The ball dropped and hit the ground in front of him. He snatched it on the hop and whirled around. Charlie M. was covering third. Carter whipped the ball to him. *Whap!* It struck Charlie M.'s glove and stuck there.

"Out!"

Carter pumped his fist once and let out a huge sigh of relief as he hustled off the field.

In the dugout, Coach Harrison was beaming. "Excellent teamwork, boys, just excellent! Now let's add a few runs to our side, huh?" He called out the new batting order, changed slightly from the start because of the substitutions made.

Carter, batting in the sixth slot and due up fourth that inning, hoped to help do just that. Instead, coming to bat with the bases loaded and no outs, he sent the ball sky high, right above the catcher. The catcher whipped off his mask and held up his glove. The ball landed safe, sound, and snug in the pocket—and Carter headed back to the bench.

Raj wasn't any more successful. He watched two pitches go by and fanned at the third.

"I didn't see one I liked," Raj said morosely as he took a seat on the bench.

Luckily, Peter, up next, did. *Pow!* Bat met ball for a low-flying drive that fell between the right and center fielders. While the outfielders moved to recover the ball, Craig dashed home from third, followed closely by Charlie S. Charlie M. stayed at third as Peter slid safely into second.

"My turn!" Ron said, hurrying to the plate. But to his obvious dismay, he popped out to end the inning.

Mid-Atlantic 5, Midwest 1.

"Two more innings, boys. We just have to hold them for two more innings!" Coach Harrison cried, his eyes snapping with excitement.

Mid-Atlantic did hold Midwest in the bottom of the fifth. Unfortunately, Midwest returned the favor, executing a crisp double play to end Mid-Atlantic's chances of adding to their final run tally. Still, Mid-Atlantic took the field at the bottom of the sixth with a comfortable four-run lead.

That lead shrank with one swing.

Ping! With a runner on first and no outs, the same moonfaced batter who'd sneaked the ball down the line past Keith now launched a rocket to deep right field. Craig raced back, then slowed to a trot. Carter didn't blame him. He didn't stand a chance at making the catch; the ball cleared the fence with room to spare.

Mid-Atlantic 5, Midwest 3.

Carter watched, muscles tense, as pitcher Peter readied himself for the next batter. It was devastating to give up a home run so late in the game. He willed Peter to put it behind him.

Peter did. He struck out the next batter in five pitches. When the one after that grounded out, Mid-Atlantic had their first victory!

"Nice job, man!" Carter congratulated Peter as they

trotted off the field after shaking hands with the Midwest players.

"Cool as a cucumber, that's what you were," Ash agreed. Then he leaned in and whispered mischievously, "Now *that's* what I call a triumph!"

CHAPTER
FIFTEEN

Mom! Dad! Melanie! Over here!"

Liam waved to his parents and sister as they made their way toward the big tent just inside The Grove. It was Saturday morning, and since West didn't play again until Sunday, the hosts had arranged for the players to spend some time with their families.

"Who've you got coming?" Liam asked Phillip as he waited for the security guard to let his family in.

"Just my mom," Phillip said. "Dad couldn't get away this year."

"Oh. Sorry."

"It's okay. He's watching at the Super Screen with

all the other Ravenna fans. Last year, they packed the place every time we played."

Super Screen was the cinema complex near where the boys lived. The management had arranged for West's games to be shown live in its biggest theater. Some of Liam's teammates from the Pythons—Spencer Park, Jay Mendoza, Scott Hoffmann, and a few others—had watched the first game there. Spencer had sent him a photo of the fans celebrating West's victory. Liam hoped they'd have more celebrations in the days ahead.

Phillip spoke again. "I wish I could be in two places at the same time tomorrow—on the field and watching the broadcast. That way, I could hear what Nathan Daly says about me right when he says it. I mean, about *us*," he corrected hastily. "What he says about *us*, not me."

Liam hid a smile at the slip. It was no secret that Phillip admired Nathan Daly; Liam had never seen him as excited as he'd been at the opening ceremonies. He could only guess how amazing it would be for Phillip to hear his idol comment on his pitching performance during a game.

Liam was about to remind him that he could watch the replay of the game anytime, but he was stopped by the joyful cry of Mrs. DiMaggio.

"Phillip! There you are! You don't mind if I steal him, do you, Liam?"

The McGraths came into the tent a moment later. Liam gave his mother and father warm hugs.

"What am I, chopped liver?" Melanie griped, tossing her dark hair over her shoulder.

Liam leaned close and sniffed. "Nooo," he mused, "more like three-day-old tuna left out in the sun. In the Sahara."

"Very funny! Just for that..." She grabbed him in a headlock and rubbed her knuckles on his scalp as he tried to squirm away.

"Now, now, Melanie," Mrs. McGrath chided mildly. "Try not to damage your brother. He's got a big game tomorrow."

"That's right; he does." Melanie released him, suddenly serious. "How're you feeling about that, anyway?"

He knew what she meant by *that*. At five o'clock the next day, West would face Mid-Atlantic.

Liam shrugged. "Okay, I guess."

"And will you be okay if Carter's on the mound?"

"If he is," Liam said, "I'll just pretend he's any other pitcher."

"Really?" Melanie sounded skeptical. "Do you think Carter will look at you like any other batter?"

"Why wouldn't he?"

The trouble was, Liam *could* think of a reason Carter might treat him differently: the strikeout last year. Carter knew how deeply it had affected Liam. He wouldn't want it to happen again. And he certainly wouldn't want to *cause* it to happen.

Will it change how he pitches to me, though? Liam wondered uneasily. He didn't think it would, but it bothered him that he didn't know for sure.

His father interrupted his thoughts. "So, Liam, we have permission to take you out to dinner tonight. I thought we'd go to that burger place we discovered last year. Sound good?"

"Sounds great!" Liam replied. The restaurant wasn't fancy, but the food had been fantastic. "Can Phillip and his mom come, too?"

His mother looked flustered. "Oh, um, I don't know, honey. It—it might be too late to get the okay for him to join us."

Liam was about to give up when Melanie jumped in. "Come on, Mom. It'll be much more fun if Phillip is there."

Mrs. McGrath shot her a look but relented. "Well, I'll see what I can do."

The DiMaggios accepted the invitation and, after

approvals were obtained from the Little League personnel, promised to meet the McGraths at the restaurant.

"This is going to be great!" Melanie said that evening in the car. Her eyes shone with excitement.

Liam stared at her. "You don't even like burgers."

"Oh, it's not the food I'm looking forward to. It's the company."

"Really? Since when do you like spending time with a couple of twelve-year-old boys?"

Instead of answering, Melanie began telling him about their old house. "Everything's so different on the inside: new carpet, new paint, my old room is an office, yours has one big bed instead of two twins. It...well, it doesn't feel like our home anymore, you know?"

Then she brightened. "But Forest Park itself looks exactly the same. And you wouldn't believe how psyched everyone is about the team making it here again. There are posters in all the store windows and a huge banner stretched above Main Street. It was like going back in time to last year except..." Her voice trailed off.

"Except this year, that's not our team," Liam finished for her.

"Yeah." She leaned closer. "Just between you and me, I—well, I really miss it here. Not that I don't like California, but—"

"This is home."

She nodded.

They pulled into the burger joint's parking lot. Inside, the hostess led them to a large table set for nine. Liam started to ask about the extra seats when someone called his name.

He turned to see a small woman with brown hair and a warm smile hurrying toward him. "Aunt Cynthia?" he said, surprised. "And Uncle Peter, hey!" he added when he saw Carter's father.

"Carter's here, too!" his aunt said as she folded him into her arms. "He stopped to use the restroom."

All at once, Liam understood why his mother had looked flustered when he'd asked to invite the DiMaggios. As far as he knew, Carter and Phillip still hadn't come face-to-face. Now they would, and with many eyes watching.

And a video camera recording the moment, too, if Melanie had her way. "Not a chance!" Liam cried when he saw his sister pulling a small piece of equipment from her bag. "Mom!"

"Melanie," Mrs. McGrath warned.

"Oh, fine," Melanie groused. "But it would have made a killer scene in my—" She broke off suddenly, her attention riveted by something near the door.

Liam looked over. His heart skipped a beat.

Phillip and his mother had just come in. At that same moment, Carter came out of the restroom. The two boys froze.

Liam turned to his parents. "Why didn't you tell me Carter was—"

Mrs. Jones touched Liam's arm. "When I heard that Phillip was coming and that Ash couldn't join us because he was going to the movies with his mother, I asked them not to. I had a feeling...Liam, look." She nodded toward the door.

Carter put out his hand. "I never congratulated you on last year's World Series win," Liam heard him say. "So...congratulations, Phillip." And then he smiled an honest-to-goodness, from-the-heart smile.

Liam held his breath—and let it out when Phillip smiled back and shook Carter's hand. "Thanks. And congrats to you on your knuckleball. I've seen you throw it on TV."

"Yeah?"

"Yeah." Phillip caught Liam watching them and laughed. "I think your cousin is a little stunned that we're being friendly."

Carter laughed, too. "You think?"

As the boys made their way to the others, the door

to the restaurant opened again. A tall man wearing a baseball cap walked in. When the man took off his cap, Liam gasped.

"Guys!" he whispered urgently. "It's Nathan Daly!"

Carter's jaw dropped. Phillip's eyes widened. Mr. Daly saw them staring and waved. A moment later, he moved toward them.

"Oh my gosh, oh my gosh, oh my gosh," Phillip said. He turned to Liam, obviously rattled. "What should I say?"

Mr. Daly had reached them by then. He gave Liam a wink and said, "How about 'hello, Nathan, happy to meet you'?"

Phillip spun around. "HelloNathanhappytomeetyou," he said in a rush.

Nathan chuckled. It was a warm, rich sound. "You boys in the tournament?"

"Yes, sir. I'm Liam McGrath. I play for West. This is my cousin Carter Jones. He plays for Mid-Atlantic."

"And I'm your number one fan!" Phillip blurted.

Everyone burst out laughing. Phillip looked mortified.

"He's Phillip DiMaggio," Liam said. "He pitches for West."

"DiMaggio, huh?" Nathan smiled. "There's a name I won't soon forget."

The remaining introductions were made, with the adults seeming just as thrilled to meet the baseball star as the boys, then Nathan excused himself. "Best of luck to you boys. And be sure to enjoy every minute of it!"

Phillip stared after him, eyes shining. "Did you hear what he said? 'A name I won't soon forget.'"

"We heard him...Number One Fan," Carter teased.

CHAPTER
SIXTEEN

Come on, man, get up!"

Carter opened one eye. Ash poked him again and said, "It's time for the most important meal of the day."

Raj sat up in the bunk bed closest to Carter. He had a terrific case of bed head and a hopeful expression. "Pizza?"

"Not pizza—*breakfast*," Ash said, rolling his eyes. "Breakfast is the most important meal of the day."

Raj yawned. "Well, since it's Sunday, and at my house Sunday breakfast is usually leftover pizza, I just figured." He yawned again and hopped down from the top bunk. "But I guess pancakes, sausage, eggs, and juice will have to do!"

Carter laughed as Raj trundled off to the bathroom. Ash didn't. He tightened his lips and shook his head. "I don't see how you guys can be so relaxed this morning, not with our biggest challenge yet waiting for us."

Carter's laughter died. With sleep still fogging his brain a little, he'd momentarily forgotten that Mid-Atlantic was scheduled to play West that afternoon. Reality came crashing down around him, and he flopped over in bed and closed his eyes.

For the first time in their lives, he and Liam would be facing each other as pitcher and batter. They had avoided talking about it last night at dinner.

When they got back to The Grove, however, Liam had taken Carter aside. "I'm going to be playing my best tomorrow. If I think for one second you're taking it easy on me..." He didn't finish the sentence. He didn't have to. Carter knew Liam would never forgive him if his cousin thought he hadn't played his best, too.

Now he tried to imagine what it would be like pitching to Liam, but he couldn't. Instead, he dwelled on the fact that only one of them would join his teammates on the field for a joyful celebration at the end. The other would return to the dorms knowing his team was one loss away from elimination.

He opened his eyes and stared at the slats of the bunk above. *Liam is my best friend. I want him to succeed.*

He sat up, swung his legs over the side of the bed, and stood. *But I want to win, too.*

"Ladies and gentlemen," the announcer cried over the loudspeaker, "welcome to the fifteenth game of the World Series! Today the West Regional champions from Ravenna, California"—he paused to allow the crowd's applause to die down—"will face the Mid-Atlantic Regional champions from Forest Park, Pennsylvania."

The last words were nearly drowned out by the raucous roars from the fans packing the bleachers and the Hill, confirming that the bulk of the spectators were there to support Mid-Atlantic.

"Whoa," Craig said, "I think there are even more people cheering for us this year than last."

"Let's make it even louder!" Raj cried. He cupped his hands around his mouth and bellowed, "Woo-hooo! Mid-Atlantic! Yeah!"

West was the home team. Carter glanced over at the first-base dugout and caught a glimpse of Liam suiting up in his catcher's gear. They had exchanged quick smiles and waves coming on and off the field during warm-ups. Seeing Liam prepare to catch for someone other than himself made Carter's spirits sag just a little. He quickly shook himself out of it.

Got to stay focused!

He saw Phillip, too, of course. He could tell from the pitcher's posture that he was in game mode.

Well, so am I, Carter thought.

A few minutes later, the West players raced onto the field for the start of the game. The crowd cheered as they threw the ball around. Then the umpire called, "Play ball!"

Freddie, Mid-Atlantic's first batter, strode to the plate.

"You got this, Freddie," Charlie M. said encouragingly. "Start us off strong!"

Freddie did—much to Carter's surprise. Not because he didn't think Freddie could hit. He just wasn't sure how Freddie would handle Phillip's pitches. But there he was on first, the proud owner of a single.

Keith grounded out to short. Craig adjusted his helmet and said, "My turn to make something happen." He squared his broad shoulders and moved to the batter's box, looking for all the world like a bulldog ready to pick a fight. He swung hard, but he sent Phillip's first two pitches foul.

"Come on, Craig, you got him, you can do it!" his teammates yelled.

Ping! The Mid-Atlantic players leaped to their feet at the sound of bat meeting ball. Craig tore down the base path as the ball flew into shallow right field behind the first baseman. Freddie took off for second.

Rodney raced in from right field. He couldn't get there in time to catch the ball, but he nabbed it after a few bounces and threw to first. Craig appeared to hit the bag a split second after the ball reached Mason's glove. Sure enough, the umpire jerked her arm backward, confirming that Craig was out. Mason cocked his arm as if to throw to second, but Freddie was already there.

The fans applauded Craig's effort as he trotted back to the dugout. Carter thought he might be disappointed, but he was beaming. "I was nervous about facing that DiMaggio guy again. Last year, his pitches seemed a lot harder to hit." Craig lowered his voice. "Plus, I kept thinking about Liam's strikeout, you know?"

Carter nodded.

"So either I'm a lot better than Liam," Craig continued, "or that guy's not such a great pitcher after all, because those pitches looked like volleyballs coming at me."

Carter stared at Craig in disbelief.

"Just you wait," Craig said. "You'll see what I mean when you get up."

The next batter was Ash. He usually hit fifth in the order, but the coaches had moved him up because his batting had been so strong. He stepped into the box and lifted the bat over his shoulder, twirling it slightly while he awaited the pitch.

On the bench, Charlie S. started clapping and chanting, "Ash. Ash. Ash." The other boys picked up the rhythm. Even Coach Harrison and Coach Filbert joined in.

Swish!

Their chant faltered with Ash's first strike, then resumed with greater intensity. "Ash! Ash! Ash!"

Swish!

Strike two. Ash stepped back, rolled his shoulders a few times, and got back into his stance.

"Ash! Ash! Ash! A—"

Swish!

The chanting, and the inning, ended when Ash struck out.

"That's okay, boys," Coach Harrison said encouragingly. "We've got at least five more chances to get on that board!"

"Nice swings, man," Carter told Ash just before he left the dugout.

Ash let out a frustrated sigh. "Those pitches were

meatballs. I should have gotten a hit. I fanned because Liam distracted me."

Carter stopped short. He wanted to ask Ash what he meant. But there wasn't time.

"Less chat, more action, Carter," Coach Harrison called. "Get on out to the mound for your warm-up throws!"

CHAPTER
SEVENTEEN

Nicely done, boys," Coach Driscoll praised the West players as they joined him in the dugout. "Now let's see if we can get some runs on the board." He rattled off the batting order. "Dom, Phillip, Matt! Then Rodney, Liam, and Mason."

"Rodney made a great stop, don't you think?" Liam commented as he sat next to Phillip.

Phillip nodded but didn't say anything or even smile. Instead, he leaned forward and stared at Carter on the mound.

"I never thanked him," he said suddenly. "I should have said something last night, but I didn't. I was too busy thinking about Nathan Daly."

Liam looked at him, puzzled.

Phillip returned his look. "He didn't have to say anything about this"—he wiped his cheek against his right shoulder—"but he did."

Then Liam understood. "Your 'tell.'"

A few weeks earlier, Melanie had accidentally sent Carter a video montage of Phillip pitching. Ash had watched the video with Carter, and he noticed that every time Phillip prepared to throw a changeup, he wiped his cheek on his shoulder. Any batter who knew about the face-wipe would know which pitch was coming.

Carter, still bearing a grudge against Phillip, had sat on the information for a few days. But his conscience got the better of him, and he explained the discovery to Liam. Liam had told Phillip—only to find out that Phillip did the face-wipe intentionally as a superstitious ritual. Since the cat was out of the bag, however, he and Liam had come up with a new plan. Instead of actually doing the move, Phillip just imagined himself going through the motions. Fortunately, it seemed to work.

"He could have used my 'tell' to his advantage," Phillip murmured now.

"He'd never do that," Liam said. "That's not the kind of guy he is."

"I wish I'd said something last night."

"You'll have another chance," Liam assured him.

"Batter up!"

Dom headed toward the plate. As usual, he hopped over the foul line, believing that stepping on it was bad luck. He needed more than luck to get a hit, though. Carter mowed him down with three straight fastballs.

"Ooo-kay," Dom said, looking dazed as he reentered the dugout. "Those weren't regular fastballs. They were lightning-fast fastballs."

Phillip picked up his bat. "I'll handle 'em," he said confidently.

He might have, too, except Carter didn't serve him any. Instead, he got Phillip out on changeups.

That brought up Matt. Easily the most muscular player on the team, Matt channeled his strength into solid hits whenever he connected. This time, though, he didn't connect. Like Dom and Phillip, he went down swinging.

As Liam strapped on his catcher's gear, Coach Driscoll approached him with Mid-Atlantic's lineup in his hand. "I thought you should see who's batting this inning." The coach showed him the order.

First up was Charlie M. Then it was Carter's turn. Liam's heart started pounding. His palms turned sweaty and his mouth turned dry. He'd known he'd be behind the plate when Carter came up to bat, just as he'd known he'd face Carter's pitches. He thought he was prepared for it. He wasn't.

What should I do? he thought as he hurried to his spot behind the plate. *Should I look at him? Not look at him? Smile? Not smile?*

He pushed the concerns from his mind when Charlie M. got into his batting stance. Charlie knocked Phillip's third pitch to Dom at shortstop. Dom threw him out at first.

Now Carter stepped into the batter's box at the right side of the plate. Their eyes met briefly. Then Carter turned to the mound and lifted the bat over his shoulder.

In that instant, Liam's game brain took over. He remembered that Carter, a lefty, used to pull the ball to the right whenever he hit it.

I should have told Coach Driscoll about that! he thought. If the coach knew, he might have repositioned the outfielders a few steps to the right.

But Liam hadn't told him, and maybe it wouldn't matter. After all, Carter could have learned how to send the ball the other way in the past few months, and if he didn't pull the ball, the West players would be out of position.

Carter's getting a hit was a distinct possibility as Phillip had not been pitching his best. Liam hoped that it was just nerves and that Phillip had worked them out by now.

He hadn't. Liam signaled for a fastball, but what Phillip threw was anything but.

Pow! Carter connected. Sure enough, the ball pulled to the right as it soared past first base and into the outfield. Applause thundered down as Carter sprinted down the base path. Liam appraised his progress.

He's faster than he was last year, he thought with a flicker of unease. *Almost Charlie Murray fast!*

But it wouldn't have mattered if Carter had been the fastest boy on the planet. Rodney caught the fly ball, and Carter was out.

A small boy—Liam thought his name was Raj— came up to bat. He barely moved as three straight pitches sailed wide of the strike zone. He let the fourth go by for a called strike and got a free ticket to first when Phillip misfired the fifth.

"Shake it off, man, shake it off!" Liam called out as he threw the ball back to Phillip.

Allen looked the first two pitches into the mitt. He swung at the third, bouncing it toward Cole. Cole fielded it cleanly and threw to Nate at second. Raj was out, and the top of the inning was over.

West hurried off as Mid-Atlantic took the field. Liam saw Carter's head turn in his direction and then quickly snap forward. That was okay; the last thing Liam wanted was to distract Carter.

In the dugout, he looked for Phillip, who usually helped him with his catcher's gear. This time the pitcher just sat down heavily on the bench.

Coach Driscoll hurried over. "Phillip, everything all right?"

Phillip rubbed his hands over his face. "I think you should take me out, Coach."

Coach Driscoll chuckled. "Because you struck out and gave up a walk last inning? I hardly think that qualifies as not playing well." He turned serious. "What would is the regret you'd feel later if you gave up on yourself now."

"You know what stinks?" Liam put in as he shed the rest of his gear, put on a helmet, and grabbed a bat. "Thinking that you have to carry the whole game yourself. You don't. We're all in this together!"

"I know something else that stinks," Dom called from across the dugout. "Dog poo. Oh, and Matt's breath after he eats buffalo chicken."

"Say what?" Matt said, swiveling his head in Dom's direction.

"It's the truth, and you know it," Dom scoffed.

"Hello?" Rodney, up first, was about to leave the dugout. "What would *really* stink is if you guys kept talking instead of cheering for me!"

CHAPTER
EIGHTEEN

Carter took his cap off, ran his forearm over his sweaty hair, and put the cap back on. He rubbed his left hand on his pant leg and took the ball out of his glove. It took willpower not to pound it back into the pocket over and over while he waited for the West batter to come to the plate. He knew that motion advertised anxiety—and he didn't want the batter to think he was anxious. So instead, he clutched the ball behind his back.

He was nervous, though, because Rodney had racked up lots of hits in the postseason. Ash knew it, too. He flashed the signal Carter was hoping for.

Knuckleball.

Carter hid his excitement and gave a curt nod. He'd

already tucked the ball against his palm in anticipation. Now he curled his fingers so the tips of the pointer, middle, and ring fingers were digging into the white cover by the stitching and the tip of the thumb was gripping below. He went into his windup, reared back, lunged forward, and threw, flicking his fingers and thumb as he released the ball.

That flick made all the difference in the knuckleball. If only the top fingers did it, the ball would spin wildly. Add in the thumb, though, and the ball scarcely rotated. Instead, it fluttered as it pushed its way through the air, resisting it.

Carter's flick was perfect. The ball looked like it was dancing as it headed toward Ash's open glove. Rodney took a big cut but missed by a mile.

Carter offered up a second knuckleball with the same result. Then, following Ash's signal, he switched to a changeup. Rodney clipped the ball for a dribbler. Carter raced in, scooped it up, and threw to first. Rodney was out.

Carter headed back to the mound. He took in a deep breath through his nose and let it out slowly through his mouth, a relaxation technique that Liam had taught him. He turned to see who the next batter was—and breathed deeply a few more times.

It was Liam.

Carter squeezed his eyes shut.

He's just another batter. He's just another batter. He's just another batter.

No, he's not, a little voice inside Carter objected. *He's your best friend. And remember what happened last year?*

An image of Liam lying in the dirt after his strike-out flashed in Carter's mind.

Then another voice spoke in his head: *"If I think for one second you're taking it easy on me…"*

"I won't, Liam," Carter said under his breath. He pushed the ball into his palm and leaned in for the signal. When it came, he blinked in surprise.

Changeup?

He shook it off with a hurried movement of his head. But Ash flashed the same fingers again. Carter bit his lip and nodded. As he moved the ball in his hand, he glanced at Liam.

His cousin was staring at him with an intensity Carter had never seen in his eyes. *Because I've never pitched to him during a game before,* he thought. He narrowed his eyes. *Not until now.*

He reared back and threw. The off-speed pitch seemed to float toward Ash's glove. Liam swung.

Pow!

It was a line shot toward third base. Allen leaped. He almost got his glove on the ball, but it fell behind him and rolled away. Fortunately, Charlie M. had dashed in from left field to back him up and was there to retrieve it. If he hadn't, the damage might have been much worse: Liam might have been standing on second instead of first.

Carter received the ball back from Charlie M. He glanced toward the first-base dugout to see who was up next. It was Mason.

As he waited for Mason to take his stance, he heard a familiar voice cry out.

"Get ready to motor, Liam!" Phillip called from the dugout.

Unlike right-handed pitchers who face third base, Carter, a southpaw, faced first. So he saw what Phillip did next: He pointed at his chest, then his nose, and stabbed his finger in the air.

Carter thought he recognized that gesture. It looked like the nose-bop Liam had pulled on Phillip at last year's World Series, like the gesture Phillip had made after striking Liam out—the one he punctuated with "Made you whiff!"

A shock wave rocketed through Carter's system. He thought Liam hated that gesture because it reminded him of the strikeout. Why would Phillip make it now? Unless...

Is it some kind of secret signal between them?

He shook his head. If it was, he couldn't waste time wondering what it meant. Instead, he faced Mason with renewed determination to make Liam's the last hit West got off him.

Mason stepped into the box. Green eyes blazing, Carter stared at him for a second. Then he went into his windup and hurled the first pitch, a heater that hit Ash's glove with a loud pop. Mason didn't even swing.

"Strike one!" the home-plate umpire cried, gesturing to the side with his fist.

Carter followed with a tailing fastball that caught the inside corner of the plate. Mason let that one go by, too.

"Strike two!"

Is he going to swing at anything? Carter asked himself.

He got his answer on the next pitch, a knuckleball with plenty of movement. To Carter, it looked like it might go wide of the strike zone. Yet Mason went for it—and struck out. When Nate also fanned on three pitches, the inning was over.

As he moved off the mound, Carter glanced back at his cousin. Liam wasn't looking his way, though; he was approaching Phillip.

"Time to show them your heat!" he heard Liam say.

Not too long ago, Carter would have bristled to hear Liam support Phillip. But not now. *They're teammates. No*...he amended, recalling the two of them joking the night before. *They're friends.*

And for the first time, that was really okay with him. What had happened in the past was no longer important. Moving forward was.

CHAPTER
NINETEEN

Okay," Phillip said in the dugout, "let's do this thing!"

Liam didn't know what had made the difference for Phillip—his teammates' support, his almost-hit off Carter's knuckleball, or just settling into the game—but he looked like a different player on the mound. His delivery was smooth and natural. His fastballs sizzled and hit Liam's glove smack in the pocket for strikes. His changeups fooled batters again and again. And Liam could personally attest to the fact that his stare-down was as intense as ever. It came as no surprise to him when Phillip retired the side in order. The West players slapped him on the back when they reached the dugout.

The bottom of the third began with a walk for Cole. Surprised, Phillip and Liam exchanged glances.

"Think your cousin is losing steam?" Phillip whispered.

"Don't count on it," Liam warned. But he wondered, too. And deep inside, a very small part of him hoped it might be true, because he wanted to leave the game a winner.

Carmen grounded out but advanced Cole to second. Dom reached first on a fielder's error and Cole dashed to third. Then Phillip knocked out a single that sent Cole home and saw Dom speeding safely to second!

The West players in the dugout went crazy. "Keep it going, Matt!" they cried as the muscular boy strode to the plate. "You can do it!"

Matt dug his toe into the dirt beside home plate, lifted the bat over his shoulder—and struck out in five pitches.

"Knuckleballs," he muttered as he came into the dugout.

Two on, two outs—and Rodney was up. He pinged a dribbler toward the mound. Carter darted forward—and flubbed the pickup! Rodney made it to first. Phillip made it to second, and Dom landed on third. If the noise in the dugout had been loud before, now it was positively deafening!

Liam's heart started pounding, but with anticipation, not fear.

As he left the dugout, however, a sudden thought struck him: *I haven't seen his knuckleball yet.* Then it was fear that made his heart beat faster.

Liam had never hit a knuckleball—at least, he didn't think he had. Back in the Regional tournament, he had faced a pitcher who struck him out on three straight knuckleballs. He had faced him again in the title game, where he saw two more floaters before launching a pitch over the fence for a game-winning homer.

But was that pitch a knuckleball? He thought it might have been. Hoped it was, because it meant he could hit the tricky pitch. But he didn't know for sure.

He eyed Carter warily. It was like looking at a stranger—an unsmiling, fiercely competitive stranger, whose stare was all business. Liam swallowed hard. His grip tightened on the bat.

Something tells me I'm about to see that knuckleball for myself right now.

He took a deep breath. Carter went through his windup and threw. The ball fluttered toward him. He kept his eye on it, swung—and missed.

"Nice try."

The murmur behind him was quiet but filled with

intensity. Liam risked a glance back, expecting to see a look of smug satisfaction on Ash's face. But the catcher simply stood up and threw the ball back to Carter before settling back into his crouch.

Carter threw again. Same pitch. Same result. Same murmured *nice try* from Ash.

Liam quickly stepped out of the box.

Is Ash trying to psych me out with that nice try *stuff?* he wondered as he tapped the dirt from his cleats. He flicked a look to the catcher again, but it was impossible to see Ash's expression behind the mask. He gripped the bat more tightly, stepped back in, and stared down at Carter.

Everything but the connection between them faded. Carter reared back, lunged forward, and threw. The ball practically danced toward the plate. Liam swung—and missed.

CHAPTER
TWENTY

I'm sorry, Liam," Carter whispered as he trotted to the dugout, his head turning to watch his cousin trudge away from the plate. "I had to do it."

With bases loaded and two outs, Carter had thrown three straight knuckleballs. His teammates were overjoyed, but he just felt lousy. He had suspected Liam would struggle with that pitch, and he'd used it against him.

But what else could I have done? he thought as he took a seat on the bench. *If I'd thrown him a fastball, he would have killed it. If I'd thrown him a changeup, he'd have killed that, too, just like he did his first at bat. And if I hadn't thrown the knuckleball, he would have killed me for taking it easy on him!*

A hand fell on his shoulder. "You okay, son?" It was Coach Harrison. He was looking at Carter with concern.

Carter stared at the ground between his feet and shrugged. He didn't trust himself to speak.

"It wasn't fair of me to put you in that situation," the coach said. "So I'm taking you out and putting Peter on the mound."

Carter's head snapped up. "What? No, Coach, it's okay! I'm okay!" Carter knew Peter was a good pitcher, but he also knew that sometimes Peter let tension get the better of him.

Coach Harrison's mind was made up, however. "There'll be other games," he said.

But how many, if we lose today? Carter wanted to scream.

"We've got to get him out of our heads once and for all."

Carter turned to find Ash standing behind him, a cup of water in his hand.

"Who?"

"Liam. Remember how I told you he distracted me in the first inning?"

Carter nodded.

"Well, it wasn't his fault. It was mine. I started thinking about the message he sent me at the parade—you know,

125

about him being okay with me catching for you." Ash drained his cup. "Anyway, I thought I should tell you...I said something to him while he was at bat this last time."

Carter tensed. "What?".

Ash shifted on his feet. "I said 'nice try' after he missed your first two pitches. I meant it in a good way," he added hurriedly. "But now I'm worried he might think I was being sarcastic or something. And that you might think it was kind of disloyal of me to, you know, offer him support."

Relief flooded through Carter. He tilted his head back to look Ash in the eye. "I don't think that," he assured the catcher. "But you're right. We both need to put Liam out of our heads whenever we play his team. Which we might not get to do again if we don't win today!"

Ash shouldered his bat and smiled. "I'll do my best to make sure we do win, then."

Both boys turned their attention to Craig at the plate. They clapped and cheered as their teammate readied himself for whatever Phillip sent his way. After one pitch, though, their applause faltered. After two, it stopped altogether. After the third, Ash made his way out of the dugout, and Carter murmured kind words to Craig when he sat down after having struck out.

If Phillip keeps throwing like this... Carter felt a little anxious until he glanced at the scoreboard. West had only one run. There was still plenty of time left. *If we get on base, we could tie things up, maybe even take the lead!*

Ash got them started at the top of the fourth, reaching first on a bouncing grounder. He hustled to second when Charlie M. also hit a grounder that hopped over the base path into the gap behind first and second. That brought up Peter for his first turn at bat. Unfortunately, his turn didn't go very well. He struck out. So did Raj.

The bottom of the fourth inning started with Mason coming up to bat. *Pow!* He clocked Peter's first pitch for a towering home run that fell out of sight behind the fence.

Carter watched as the scoreboard changed from WEST 1, MID-ATLANTIC 0 to WEST 2, MID-ATLANTIC 0.

Nate, the second West batter, singled. But he didn't get any farther than first because James, in for Cole at third and taking his spot in the batting order, too, hit into a double play. Then Elton, in for Carmen in center field, got a free ride to first when Peter threw four balls in a row. Ash took a moment to talk to his pitcher. Whatever he said must have helped because Peter struck Dom out.

Mid-Atlantic might have been down, but they were far from out. The top of the fifth started off with a bang—or rather, a *ping* with a single off Allen's bat. When Charlie S.—now in Ron's spot—got a single, too,

Carter's spirits soared with hope. That hope didn't even fade when Stephen, in for Freddie, struck out.

"We're on base," he murmured, drumming his fists on his thighs. "Now we just need one good hit."

Luke had subbed in for Keith and now came up to the plate. He delivered just what they needed, crushing one of Phillip's pitches for a double that scored Allen and Charlie!

"Yes! Tie ball game!" Carter cheered. He slapped a double high five with Ash.

Craig looked to add more to their side of the board with a high fly to center field. Luke took off for third. But Craig's blast was caught for out number two—and when Luke couldn't get back to second before the throw, the top of the inning was over.

The game didn't stay tied for long. With two outs and Rodney on first, Liam came up to bat. He took a huge cut at Peter's second pitch—and walloped it for a triple!

The fans roared with appreciation for the blast. Carter, meanwhile, was torn between wanting to add his voice to theirs and wishing the ball had been caught. When Mason followed with a single that got Liam across home plate, though, any thought of cheering vanished.

Two runs were all the West players earned that inning as the next batter grounded out.

Mid-Atlantic threatened to answer those runs right away. Ash smashed a double. He reached third on a single from Charlie M. Peter hit into a double play, sending Charlie M. back to the dugout with him.

C'mon, Raj, Carter urged silently. *Keep us alive.*

But Raj struck out.

Final score: West 4, Mid-Atlantic 2.

An hour later, Carter was showered and heading to meet his parents, who were waiting for him. His mother enveloped him in a warm embrace.

"Oh, honey, I'm so sorry," she whispered. "I know it couldn't have been easy to face Liam. But it's only one loss. You'll get wins from here on out, I'm sure."

Carter pulled back and smiled. "I'm okay, Mom, really."

She studied his face for a moment and hugged him again.

Mr. Jones ruffled his hair. "So aside from today, how have things been going? You getting to see much of Liam?"

Carter seesawed his hand. "Not as much as I'd like, but some."

"Well, don't worry, you'll have plenty of time together at Christmas."

Carter wrinkled his nose in confusion. "Huh?"

Mrs. Jones gave her husband a light smack on the arm. "You weren't supposed to say anything!" she admonished.

"Say anything about what?" Carter demanded to know.

"Liam and his family are spending the holidays with us this year," his mother told him. Carter gave a whoop that drew curious looks from his teammates.

"Now come on," Mrs. Jones said, "I want to thank Ash's mother again for letting the McGraths use her house."

The three of them made their way toward Ash and Mrs. LaBrie but stopped short when they heard Ash say, "Surprise? What surprise?"

The suspicious look on his face told Carter that Ash didn't think the surprise was going to be something he liked.

But Mrs. LaBrie just beamed and said, "If I told you, it wouldn't be a surprise, would it? You'll just have to wait and find out with everyone else! Oh, hello, Cynthia, Peter! And, Carter, how are you?"

He assured her that he was fine. When the parents started chitchatting, he nudged Ash. "What's going on?" he whispered.

Ash scowled. "I don't know for sure, but if I had to guess"—his scowl deepened—"I'd say we're moving again."

CHAPTER
TWENTY-ONE

Liam scanned the rec room, his gaze roaming from the boys playing video games to those at the pin-trading table to the ones lounging on the big couches, watching a movie on the wide-screen TV. Phillip and Rodney were both there, but he wasn't looking for them. He was looking for Carter.

It was late Sunday night, and he hadn't seen his cousin since the game. He was half-hoping, half-dreading to see him now. Hoping, because he wanted to be sure his best friend was okay. Dreading, because he was afraid his best friend might not be.

Instead of Carter, however, he spotted Ash. The

blond-haired boy was tapping a Ping-Pong ball into the air with a paddle. He looked upset.

Well, duh, Liam thought. *His team lost today.*

Yet instinct told him that Ash was troubled by something more than the loss. *Carter has always said Ash is a fierce competitor. Of course he has to be bummed out. But I would have bet anything on him putting it behind him and gearing up to face the next challenge.*

Besides, there was no way Coach Harrison would have let any of his players dwell on the loss. No, something else was going on. Liam was sure of it.

Pink-pink-pink-pink-pink. Ash had mis-hit the ball, sending it bouncing across the room toward Liam. Liam bent down and grabbed it. When he straightened, he saw Ash staring at him.

Liam walked over. "Hey," he said, handing Ash the ball.

"Hey," Ash mumbled.

Liam picked up a paddle. "Wanna play?"

Ash shrugged. "Sure."

Liam moved to one end of the table and Ash to the other. They began hitting back and forth, neither saying a word until Liam missed a return.

"You guys face Great Lakes tomorrow afternoon, right?" Liam asked as he retrieved the ball and sent it back across the net.

"Yeah."

"I'll be rooting for you."

"Thanks." Ash hit the ball into the net. He nabbed it before it dropped to the floor but didn't resume playing. "Good game today."

"You, too. Like I said before, you and Carter make a good team."

Ash put down his paddle. "Yeah. Too bad we won't be playing together after this tournament."

Liam blinked. "Why not?"

Ash sighed. "I'm probably moving again." His mouth twisted into a mirthless smile. "So if you want your old room back, it should be available soon."

"Oh." Liam was still digesting that information when Carter appeared. His cousin looked a little taken aback seeing the two of them together.

"So," Carter said, hurrying over, "what's going on here?"

"Don't worry, Carter," Liam said. "We're fine."

"I told Liam his room is going to be up for grabs again," Ash put in.

None of them said anything for a long moment. Then Liam gave a little laugh.

"What's so funny?" Ash asked.

"I was thinking about how that room has connections

to so many of us," Liam replied. "Carter and I used to hang out there all the time. Then I moved away and you moved in. You met Carter. I met Sean and Rodney. Now Sean is staying in that same bedroom, too."

He shook his head. "And the weirdness goes on! Carter met Phillip. Carter didn't like Phillip, which meant when I met Phillip, I didn't like him, either." As he spoke, his voice rose, drawing the attention of other boys in the rec room, including Rodney and Phillip.

"Someone talking about us?" Rodney said, coming to the Ping-Pong area with Phillip right behind him.

Liam pointed at Phillip. "How weird was it to find out I'd moved to your town?"

"Very," Phillip said. He grinned. "I couldn't stand the thought of you, actually."

"Likewise, I'm sure!" Liam retorted but smiled, too. He turned to Ash. "Let's face it, you and I couldn't stand the thought of each other, either, right? But now look at us, four guys—well, five if you count Rodney—"

"Which why wouldn't you?" Rodney asked, making the others laugh.

"The five of us here," Liam finished, "hanging out as friends. So what brought us together? Baseball, that's what!"

His arm swept in a wide arc. "These ballplayers and the ones on the field and in the dorms and wherever else they are come from all over the world." His voice rose even louder. "Which means that no matter where in the world we are, or go, or end up, there could be a baseball team waiting for us to join. Or coach. Or ump. Or just watch! Right?"

"Right!"

The cry came from many boys in the room. Even those who didn't speak English seemed to understand that Liam was saying something important as they grinned and pumped their fists.

"Any one of these guys could be a future teammate. Or future rival. Or"—he nodded at Ash—"a future friend. If you do move, Ash, baseball will be there to help you make friends again."

Carter put his arm around Ash's shoulders. "You'll always have your old friends, too." Ash looked from face to face and grinned. Then he held up his paddle. "Anyone want to play a different game for a change?"

In no time, they organized a doubles Ping-Pong tournament. They invited all the boys in the room to join and, in the spirit of Little League, paired U.S. players with International players. Liam teamed up with Jon, the Australian boy they'd met at the pool. Carter paired with Kita Hiro; at one point, Liam heard him ask the boy to teach him some Japanese phrases.

Some of the games were competitive; others were total wipeouts. But all the games were played with lots of laughter.

Before long, Ping-Pong was replaced with lively, good-natured pin trading. Rodney, whose collection was by far the smallest, exchanged two California theme park pins for a colorful "spinner" owned by Antonio, an outfielder from Mexico. Antonio grinned as Rodney flicked the pin's tiny metal arrow to make it move—then passed him another, simpler pin, saying in accented but very clear English, "Please, have this one, too!"

Delighted, Rodney accepted the gift and then whipped out his phone. He threw his arm around Antonio and snapped a photo of them together. He got Antonio's contact information and sent him a copy of the picture.

"Now you can get in touch with me whenever you want. Except when I'm playing!" he joked.

Later, as Liam brushed his teeth before bed, he knew that no matter how West fared in the days ahead, he would always remember the night as a highlight of the tournament.

CHAPTER
TWENTY-TWO

The days and games that followed flew by. Knowing that one more loss would mean elimination, the Mid-Atlantic players buckled down and played their best.

On Monday, they faced Huxley, Michigan, the Great Lakes Regional champion. Pennsylvania won in a landslide, 10–2, thanks to terrific hitting and heads-up play in the field.

Monday's victory was followed by another on Tuesday, this time against the Southwest team from Lone Peak, Colorado. While the 7–5 score wasn't as lopsided as the previous game, the win put Mid-Atlantic one giant step closer to earning a berth in the U.S. Championship.

Wednesday was a day off for Mid-Atlantic. After a morning practice and time in the batting cages after lunch, the team went to watch the four o'clock International game between Australia and Asia-Pacific.

"This should be a great game," Ash commented as he, Carter, their teammates, and their coaches found seats together in Lamade Stadium.

Carter agreed. For one thing, it was a beautiful afternoon, sunny and hot with very little humidity. For another, if their previous games were any indication, the teams on the field promised to give strong performances. And, finally, the winner would advance to the International Championship, just one step away from the World Series title game.

"You rooting for one of them?" Raj asked Carter.

Carter hesitated before answering. He didn't want to seem like he was playing favorites, but—"I guess I'd like to see Australia win. I've hung out with one of their players, Jon Burns, and he seems like a great guy. Plus, with Little League Baseball getting so popular in their Region, I think it's cool they're doing so well. They'd have to be to get here. But still, I read one article that called them the 'underdogs from Down Under.'"

"Japan has always been my favorite International

team," Craig put in. "I like that tradition they have of scooping dirt off the mound after they win the World Series and the respect they show to their coaches at all times."

"Well," Charlie M. joked, "we'll just have to make sure they go home with clean hands if we face them in the title game. As for me, I've always liked our neighbors to the north."

When the other boys looked at him in confusion, he clarified, "Canada! I have a connection to that country. My grandfather was from Ontario."

"Isn't that the airport the players from West and Northwest flew out of?" Raj asked, sounding puzzled.

"That airport is in Ontario, *California*," Charlie M. said with an elaborate eye roll. "I'm talking about the province of Ontario, *Canada*. You know, where Toronto is?"

Raj seemed even more baffled. "The Lone Ranger's sidekick lives in *Canada*?"

"Not Tonto, To-RON-to!" Charlie M. said in exasperation while the other boys laughed. "Oh, never mind."

Raj caught Carter's eye. He winked mischievously, letting Carter know he'd only been pretending to be clueless. Carter laughed even harder.

The game began a little while later. Australia was the home team. Jon Burns was at shortstop. The other boys Carter had met in the pool weren't starting, but he knew he'd see them play at some point.

Asia-Pacific started off strong with a pair of singles. The runners didn't score, however, because the next three batters made outs. Australia, on the other hand, saw two runners cross home plate in the first inning thanks to back-to-back walks and a double from Jon Burns.

Even though he wanted Australia to win, Carter felt bad for the Asia-Pacific pitcher. "What would you say to him if you were his coach?" he asked Coach Harrison.

"That it's just one inning and it's over and done with, so he should put it behind him," the coach replied without hesitation. "And I'd remind him that he's not the only player on the field. The inning's results do not fall just on his shoulders."

"I hope his coach tells him something like that," Carter said.

Coach Harrison smiled. "I'm sure he will."

The second inning went by scoreless for both teams. In the top of the third, Asia-Pacific's bats started talking. They racked up three runs before Australia retired the side.

The Australian boys tried but failed to close the gap. The score at the end of the third inning remained Asia-Pacific 3, Australia 2. That's where it stayed for the next two innings, too.

"Leading off for Asia-Pacific," the game announcer intoned, "Li-Chung Wu!"

Carter leaned forward. Wu had clocked a double in the third inning that scored two of his teammates. He was superquick, too, not just on the base paths but in the outfield, where he seemed to fly over the green grass. This at bat, though, he didn't need speed because the Australian pitcher grazed him with the ball. Wu dropped his bat and trotted to first.

The pitcher, meanwhile, shook his head, clearly upset with himself. He seemed to get over it, though, for he struck out the next batter. The third belted a line drive between first and second. Wu raced to second, touched the bag, and kept going, landing safely at third.

"Hoo, boy," Carter muttered. Things weren't looking good for Australia. If the next Asia-Pacific player got a decent hit, Wu would probably score.

Ping!

The batter knocked a grounder toward third. The third baseman sprinted in to meet it. The left outfielder ran to cover the bag. The third baseman scooped up the ball, checked Wu on third, and then relayed it to second. The moment the ball left his hand, however, Wu took off. The second baseman got the runner out and immediately threw to home. The throw was high! The catcher had to leap for it. He made the catch but was out of position. Wu scored.

"Oh, man, that was tough," Ash said, shaking his head in sympathy for a fellow catcher.

Australia got the next batter out to end the inning. Now they had one last chance to add to their side of the scoreboard. If the difference in score had been a single run, Carter thought they might be able to tie it up and send the game into extra innings. But with the score 4–2? He wasn't so sure.

His hope for an Australian win went up a notch, though, when the first two batters singled. Then Jon headed to the plate.

"Here you go, Jon! You got it!" Carter yelled.

Jon watched the first pitch zip by for a called strike. He let the second one pass, too. When that was ruled a strike as well, he quickly stepped out of the box. Bouncing on his toes, he shook out his arms and tilted his head from side to side. The moves looked like a ritual to Carter, something Jon did to help him get loose and focused. If so, he hoped it worked, for Australia's sake.

Jon got back into position. The pitcher wound up and threw. Jon swung. *Pow!*

Carter and his teammates leaped to their feet. Carter tracked the high fly ball as it soared through the blue sky—and dropped behind the fence! With that blast, Australia pocketed the win, 5–4.

When Carter saw Jon in the dining hall that night, he made a beeline for him. "Congratulations, man! That walk-off homer was amazing!"

Jon blushed to the roots of his blond hair at the praise and grinned with happiness. "Ta, Carter," he replied. Carter had learned that *ta* was the same as *thanks*. "I have to admit, it felt good. Felt bad for the Asia-Pacific players, though, you know?"

Carter nodded his understanding. "You going to the U.S. game tonight?"

"Nah, I'm spent. If I watch, it'll be in the rec room. You?"

"Liam's playing, so I'm going to Lamade."

"Oh, right! If you see him, tell him I'll be barracking for him!"

"Um, what?"

Jon laughed. "Sorry, I keep forgetting you don't speak Strine," he replied, meaning Australian lingo. "*Barrack* means to cheer."

"In that case, I'll tell him!"

Carter didn't see Liam before or after the game, however. But he "barracked" for his cousin through six innings. And when the game ended with West beating the New England team from Massasoit, Massachusetts, 8–5, he whipped out his phone and sent him an excited text.

Doofus! You're in the U.S. Championship!

CHAPTER
TWENTY-THREE

Liam waited all day Thursday and into the night before responding to Carter's text.

Dork! his reply read. *You're in the U.S. Championship, too!*

Earlier that day, Mid-Atlantic had defeated New England, 6–4. The Mid-Atlantic players had looked so in sync right from the first inning that Liam had figured the outcome would be in their favor. As Liam typed the words, their significance sank in.

For the second year in a row, he and Carter were both in the U.S. Championship.

Phillip, Charlie M., and Craig were returning, too, of course, but he wasn't thinking about them. He was thinking about what it was going to be like to face Carter, and the fact that one of them would advance to the World Series game, while the other would have to be satisfied with a consolation game against the team that lost the International Championship.

There were no games scheduled for Friday in case there were any rainouts. Saturday, however, was chock-full, starting at 10:30 with the Challenger Game. As fans filled the stands of Volunteer Stadium, the players—some in wheelchairs, others on crutches or holding canes, and others with developmental challenges—made their way onto the field. Most of the Little League teams attended this game. Many of the players sat with their teammates, but some joined their families.

As he made his way into the stands, Liam waved to several boys from International teams. The Australian and Japanese players weren't there; they were readying themselves for the International Championship game, which was scheduled to start at twelve thirty.

Liam took a seat, keeping an eye out for Carter and their families. Before the game, he'd been wondering what to say when he saw him. "Good luck"? "May the best team win"? Nothing seemed right.

Then Coach Driscoll offered him and the other West players a suggestion: "Put the U.S. Championship out of your minds this morning. Don't talk about it. Don't even think about it," he said. "Just be friends enjoying a ball game together."

Coach Driscoll's advice sounded good to Liam. So when Carter sat down next to him a few minutes later, he passed it on. Carter seemed relieved and instantly agreed to not discuss the upcoming game, either.

"Dudes!" Sean thundered his way up the stands and plopped down between his brother and Phillip.

Liam had been looking forward to seeing Sean. He almost didn't recognize him, though, because he wasn't wearing his typical outfit of food-stained T-shirt and gym shorts. Instead, he had on a short-sleeved polo shirt and khaki shorts. His red hair was combed smooth, and his socks matched, which was also unusual for him.

Rodney apparently thought so as well. "What's with the getup?"

"What, is it a crime to look nice?" Sean retorted.

"No, but it does make me suspect you're up to no good."

Sean turned his back on his brother and greeted Liam.

"So, how do you like my old neighborhood?" Liam asked.

"It's a really cool area," Sean replied enthusiastically. "I've been seeing a lot of it because I've been taking Lucky Boy for walks," he added with a nod at Carter. Lucky Boy was Carter's dog. "Or I guess I should say he's been taking me for walks because I let him lead the way. We went to this one place way back in the woods behind your houses. It was like a little cave beneath a rock overhang. You know the place I mean?"

Liam exchanged a smile with Carter. "Yeah. We found it a long time ago. We call it the hideout. No one else knows about it"—he lowered his voice—"not even our parents. We used to go there when we wanted to get away from everyone, you know?"

"Dude, you busted in on their secret hangout!" Rodney chastised.

Sean looked apologetic. "Oh, man, I'm sorry."

Carter laughed. "That's okay. I showed it to Ash already anyhow. But don't tell anyone else."

"Um..." Now Sean looked guilty. "Someone else might have seen it."

Liam gave Sean a horrified look. "Not my sister!"

"No, no! Her." Sean pointed to a girl on the field. She had a long brown ponytail sticking out of the back of her baseball cap. The "buddy" was busy assisting one of the Challenger players.

"That's Rachel Warburton," Carter said. "Don't worry about telling her. She's cool. But how'd you meet her?"

"She stopped by your house earlier this week. I was on my way out with Lucky Boy. She came with." Sean started fiddling with the buttons of his shirt.

"That's it!" Rodney suddenly exclaimed. "She's why you're all dressed up! You *like* her!"

"What? No! Like her? No way!" Sean protested. But his beet-red face said otherwise, making the other boys crack up.

"Hey, look, there's Mr. Delaney," Carter said, indicating a tall man with dark hair and hawk-like features. He leaned forward to direct his next comment to Phillip. "He's the one who taught me how to throw the knuckleball. And that's his son, Matt, in the wheelchair. Matt's one of the Challenger Division coaches."

The game started a short while later. Rachel stood with the leadoff batter, a girl with thick glasses. When the girl connected with a pitch, she and Rachel jumped up and down with excitement. Then Rachel took her hand and led her down the base path to first base. Both girls' smiles were radiant.

That's how baseball should be, Liam thought as he followed their progress. *No snarkiness, no getting upset when you muff a play or strike out. Just... happy to be playing.* He decided that from now on, he'd do his best to play that way.

He and his teammates watched the game, then made their way next door to Lamade for the International final. The game promised to be a nail-biter. It lived up to its promise, too, going four scoreless innings. Then, in the bottom of the fifth inning, the stalemate ended with two powerful hits.

Pow! Nigel, one of the Australian boys Liam had met at the pool, laced a line drive that whizzed past the pitched and between the second baseman and shortstop. Both the centerfielder and the left fielder raced in to get the ball as it bounced through the grass. Then both stopped short, heads turned toward each other.

Liam knew in an instant what had happened. Each outfielder thought the other was going to make the play!

A split second later, the centerfielder charged in, scooped up the ball, and threw to second. But he was too late. Nigel slid in under the tag.

"Safe!" the umpire called.

From where he sat, Liam could see the center fielder's shoulders sag. The right fielder turned away as he returned to his spot. But then he turned back, ran to his upset teammate, and patted him on the shoulder. The center fielder looked up and nodded. Both boys hurried to their positions. The center fielder pounded his fist into his glove a few times and then readied himself for the next pitch.

Good for you, Liam thought. *Put it aside and get ready for—*

Ping!

Liam leaped to his feet at the sound of bat meeting ball. He tracked the ball as it soared high and deep into left field—and then applauded with the rest of the fans as it dropped out of reach behind the fence. He didn't know the boy who had hit the homer, but he could easily imagine what his face looked like just then: one enormous smile!

Those runs proved to be the only two of the game. Try as they might, the players from Japan could not get a runner across home plate.

Final score: Australia 2, Japan 0.

An hour after the International game concluded, the West and Mid-Atlantic teams arrived at Lamade for the U.S. Championship. The crowds had swelled to capacity, covering the Hill with chairs, blankets, picnic baskets, and banners, and squeezing into every available seat in the bleachers. The afternoon sun filtered through thin cloud cover, providing lots of light but few shadows and no glare. The red dirt, groomed and wetted down between games, made a sharp contrast with the freshly painted baselines. The infield and outfield grass had been mowed to turf height the day before, and any stray debris had long since been removed.

Suddenly, the music that had been playing stopped, and the loudspeaker crackled. A hush fell over the stadium. Dugout, the Little League mascot, stopped his antics to listen.

"Ladies and gentlemen," the announcer's voice boomed, "and Little League fans the world over, welcome to the United States Championship of the Little League Baseball World Series!"

CHAPTER
TWENTY-FOUR

When Coach Harrison had announced the lineup earlier, Carter had to hide his disappointment. He wasn't starting on the mound. Then the coach had taken him aside and explained why.

"If we had won this game last year, you wouldn't have been able to pitch in the World Series title game because of your pitch count. This year, I want to be sure that if we win today, you're set to take the mound. So I'm saving you for the final innings of this game."

A thrill had shot up Carter's spine. Little League rules prohibited pitchers from taking the mound the next day if they threw more than twenty pitches in a game. Knowing the coach's plan made Carter much happier to be starting at third.

He was happier still that Mid-Atlantic had won the coin toss. As the home team, they would have the final turn at bat. If they were behind in the sixth inning...

He shook his head. *Don't even think that*, he admonished himself. *Believe.*

West took to the field first. Carter noted that Phillip wasn't the starting pitcher, either, but was stationed at third base. After West's time was up, the Mid-Atlantic players took the field for their pregame warm-ups.

Just as they were finishing, Carter heard his name called. He turned to see Liam grinning at him from the third-base dugout.

"Hey, dork, didn't you forget something?" Liam held up a fist.

Carter grinned back and held up his fist, too. They fist-bumped the air three times. "See you out there, doofus," Carter said. With excitement spreading through his veins, he hurried off to join his teammates in the dugout behind first base.

The game began. Luke was on the mound for Mid-Atlantic. Ash was behind the plate. Keith was at first, Freddie at second, Raj at shortstop, and Carter at third. Manning the outfield were Charlie M. in left, Peter in center, and Craig in right. Substitutes Ron, Charlie S., Allen, and Stephen were in the dugout, cheering along with the crowd.

First up for West was shortstop Dom. Carter pounded his fist into his glove and shouted, "Here you go, Luke!"

Carter heard Liam and the other West players encouraging their teammate, too. He blocked them out and focused.

Luke went into his windup and threw. Dom swung and missed.

"Yes!" Carter murmured.

Dom connected with the next pitch, a grounder that bounded through the grass right to Freddie. He fielded it cleanly and sent the ball to Keith's outstretched glove for out number one.

Phillip was up next. He looked three pitches into Ash's mitt. Two were balls and one a called strike. He swung at the fourth and missed. With the count two-and-two, he took a big cut at the next pitch.

Pow! It was a line drive right back at the mound. Luke had a split second to react. He stuck out his glove as he ducked. *Whap!* Amazingly, the ball landed smack in the pocket!

For a moment, Luke looked confused. Then, realizing

what he'd done, he grinned. He ended the inning with a three-pitch strikeout on Matt.

"Huddle up, boys, huddle up!" Coach Harrison called. When the players were gathered in a circle, he said, "Now let's hear it!"

"Mid-Atlantic, one-two-three! Mid-Atlantic, one-two-three!"

"Go start us off, Freddie," Coach Filbert added.

Freddie gave him a nervous nod and hurried to the plate. He ticked three pitches foul and missed the fourth for the first out. Keith and Craig both grounded out.

"And with the score zero to zero, that brings us to the conclusion of the first inning," the announcer reminded the crowd.

Rodney started things off for West in the second inning with a crushing double. Then Liam knocked out a single that got past Raj and sent Rodney to third. Mason got a hit, too. As the ball bounced just out of Freddie's reach into the outfield, Rodney ran for home like he was being chased by wolves. Liam stopped at second and Mason stood at first.

That run was all West put on the board that inning. Nate struck out and then Christopher hit into a double play.

"Okay, boys, now it's our turn to get runs on the

board," Coach Harrison said. He handed Ash a helmet and gave him a thumbs-up as he selected a bat.

"You get on base," Charlie M. called as Ash headed to the plate, "and I'll hit you home!"

Ash did as Charlie M. requested, leading off with a single. Charlie M. couldn't get him home. Instead, he got on base with a walk.

That brought up Carter. So far in the tournament, he hadn't been much of a threat at the plate. He jogged to the box now, giving himself a quick pep talk.

You can do this, he thought. *Just focus on the ball and swing!*

Just before he stepped into the box, he glanced at Liam. Unlike Carter, Liam was a powerful hitter. Suddenly, something his cousin had once said about his own hitting flashed through Carter's mind: "I imagine I'm a spring, wound tight and ready to go. Hit the release button and *wham!* I uncoil and hit that pill out of the park!"

Carter had often tried to visualize that same thing when hitting. It hadn't worked for him, so he'd given it up. Now as he hefted the bat over his shoulder—

Try it again! a small voice urged him.

Elton wound up and threw. Carter uncoiled. *Ping!* The ball flew just over Phillip's head and rolled fair. As Nate raced to nab it, Ash motored toward third. He hit the dirt and slid to the bag with time to spare. Charlie M. reached second. Carter, breathing hard and silently rejoicing, stood at first.

It worked! he thought jubilantly. *It really worked!*

Carter had time to catch his breath as Raj, up next, fouled five in a row before striking out. Peter also made an out with a pop-up that landed in Elton's glove.

Come on, Luke, Carter thought as he watched his fellow pitcher head to the plate. Luke let one go by. Then another. Then—*pow!* He laced the third between first and second! Ash scored. So did Charlie M. Carter obeyed the third-base coach and held up at second. But Freddie grounded out, so he didn't get any farther that inning.

The score changed again in the third inning.

Mid-Atlantic 2, West 1. Elton pounded Luke's fastball into deep center field. Peter dashed to make the catch but couldn't get under it. By the time the ball reached the infield, Elton was safe on third.

"Come on, Dom, bring me in!" Elton cried.

Not to be outdone, Carter bellowed, "Stay tough, Luke, stay tough!"

Elton took off for home when Dom hit a grounder that found a hole between Keith and Freddie. By the time Craig got to it, Elton was crossing the plate.

Things went from bad to worse for Mid-Atlantic

after that. Phillip got a single that moved Dom from first to second. That brought up Matt. Matt had struck out to end the top of the first inning. This time, he smacked a line drive into the gap for a double. Dom scored, but Phillip was held up at third.

Carter suppressed a groan when he saw that the next batter was Rodney. A power hitter, Rodney was always a threat at the plate.

Luke's pitch was low, but Rodney went for it anyway, swinging the bat like a golf club and launching the ball skyward above third. It disappeared in the clouds for a second before Carter caught sight of it.

"Mine!" Carter yelled. Glove overhead, he kept his eyes glued on the ball as it began its descent. He made the catch and immediately pulled out the ball, ready to throw if necessary. But Phillip and Matt hadn't moved. Carter returned the ball to Luke.

Now Liam came to the plate. A split second too late, Carter saw the look on his face. He knew that look. Heart racing, he whirled around and motioned to the outfielders.

"Move back! Move back!"

But his warning was too late.

Wham!

CHAPTER
TWENTY-FIVE

Liam watched the ball soar as he raced down the base path. When he touched first, he knew.

A three-run homer! West 6, Mid-Atlantic 2!

He rounded second and headed to third.

Carter was standing by the bag, hands on hips and head lowered. Liam's heart sank a little when he saw his cousin's posture. As he neared, Carter turned away as if to ignore him. But at the same time, he lifted his arm for a high five. Liam happily slapped his best friend's hand. He charged to home plate and jogged to the dugout, where his teammates mobbed him.

West didn't add any more runs that inning, and

Mid-Atlantic closed the four-run gap in the bottom of the third.

Keith reached first on a fielder's error. He advanced to second when Craig walked. Ash strode to the plate wearing a look of fierce determination. He let the first pitch go by. He must have liked the next one because he took a big cut at it—and clobbered it into center field!

The ball hit the grass and rolled. Christopher darted in to scoop it up. Liam leaped to his feet. "Here! Here!" he cried, positioning himself to catch the relay from the cutoff man. But the ball didn't get to him in time and first Keith and then Craig scored. Ash reached second and looked eager to go to third but wisely stayed put instead.

Coach Driscoll pulled Elton from the mound and put Carmen in in his place. Carmen took his warm-up pitches, and the home-plate umpire called, "Batter up!"

Carmen pitched carefully to Charlie M., who popped out. Liam watched out of the corner of his eye as Carter approached the plate. The last time the two teams met, Carter had pulled the ball to the right.

Coach Driscoll must have remembered Carter's hit, too; he waved his outfielders a few steps to the right.

Liam shifted in his crouch, relieved—until he saw Carter smile. For one panicked moment, he thought the coach had made a big mistake in repositioning the outfield. He shook his head.

No. Better safe than sorry. Besides, if anyone can catch up to an out-of-reach ball, it's Rodney!

As it turned out, the outfielders' position didn't matter because Carmen hit Carter on the arm with his first pitch.

"Arrrhhh!" Face contorted in pain, Carter dropped the bat and hunched over, grabbing his arm.

"Carter!"

Liam jumped up. The blood drained from his face. Carmen's fastballs were incredibly powerful, but occasionally wild. Hearing his cousin moan, Liam feared that the arm was broken. He stood by helplessly while the umpire and a medical trainer took Carter to the side. Coach Harrison raced out of the dugout, and they huddled together.

Finally, Carter straightened up and nodded.

"I'm okay, really, I'm fine," he said repeatedly. He looked straight at Liam and said once more, "I'm fine. It's just bruised."

Only then did Liam's heart start beating regularly again.

Carter shot Liam a smile and trotted off to first base to thunderous applause.

Carmen appeared shaken by the incident. Instead of throwing his usual heat, his next pitch was a meatball. Raj responded with a blast to left field. Luckily for West, it was an easy catch for Nate. When Peter grounded out to first, the chance for Mid-Atlantic to add to its score was eliminated.

"After three, the score stands West, six, Mid-Atlantic, four," the announcer proclaimed. "These changes for Mid-Atlantic: Now at first base is Stephen Kline. At third is Allen Avery. Ron Davis is in center. Charlie Santiago is in right," the announcer said.

Liam expected to hear that Carter was going in for Luke. When the substitution wasn't made, he wondered why.

Would Coach Harrison not have him pitch at all this game? With so much on the line, that seemed crazy.

Maybe he's saving him until the last inning so he can pitch tomorrow—which he'll only do if Mid-Atlantic wins, which they're not going to. The idea that the coach was keeping Carter in reserve seemed more likely.

Another thought pushed into his head then. *If Coach Harrison doesn't play him in the fifth or sixth, I won't have to face him—or his knuckleball.*

He shoved the thought away, angry with himself for worrying about the pitch. *If he's on the mound, I'll just try my best.* Then he grinned, suddenly remembering a movie quote from *Star Wars* he and Carter used often: "Do, or do not. There is no try."

Luke struck out two of the four West batters in the top of the fourth to keep the score at West 6, Mid-Atlantic 4. That's where it was when the inning ended, too, since the West players retired the side one-two-three.

Back in the dugout, Liam hurried out of his catcher's gear. He was up second, after Rodney. With a home run under his belt, he had a good feeling about his chances at the plate this time, too. He had just put on a batting helmet when the announcer reported another change to Mid-Atlantic's lineup.

"Now on the mound," the voice boomed, "Carter Jones."

CHAPTER
TWENTY-SIX

Carter's heart had given a leap when Coach Harrison told him he was replacing Luke. Then the coach had laid a hand on his shoulder.

"You're about to face your friends out there," he'd said. "But while you're on the mound, think of them as batters. Or whatever you need to imagine them to be to pitch your best."

"I will," Carter promised.

Adrenaline surged through his system as he ran onto the field and took his warm-up pitches. Now he prepared to channel it into his real pitches. He twirled the baseball in his hand, feeling the familiar rough stitching and smooth leather on his fingers.

Rodney came up to bat. They had shared some good times off the field in the past couple of days. But neither one was laughing now.

Ash flashed the signal for a fastball. Carter wound up and delivered. Rodney swung and missed.

"Strike one!" the umpire shouted.

Ash signaled for a changeup. Carter adjusted his grip, reared back, lunged forward, and threw. Rodney made contact this time, but the ball flew foul past the third-base line.

"Strike two!"

Allen retrieved the ball and returned it to Carter. Carter leaned forward, eyes on Ash's fingers. When Ash motioned for another fastball, he gave a curt nod—and then hurled one of the fastest pitches he'd ever thrown.

Rodney's swing was a fraction of a second too late.

"Strike three!"

Carter blew out a deep breath. Rodney was always a danger at the plate. Retiring him in three pitches felt good.

Liam stepped into the box. Carter's grip on the ball tightened. Then the coach's words came back to him. He relaxed.

I'm a pitcher. He's a batter. It's as simple as that.

He stared down at Ash, waiting for the signal. Ash

flicked his fingers. *Knuckleball.* Carter bit his lip. No doubt Liam would be expecting that pitch.

But even if he is, he thought, *he might not be able to hit it.*

He changed his grip so the tips of his fingers and thumb were digging into the ball's surface, wound up, and threw. It was a perfect delivery. He could barely follow the ball as it fluttered toward Ash's glove. Then—

Pow!

Liam creamed it! Carter whipped around as the small white sphere soared high over the infielders' heads toward left field. Charlie M. raced back until he couldn't go any farther. Liam touched first and dashed to second. Charlie M. raised his glove. Liam hit second and kept going. Charlie M. gave a mighty leap—and plucked the ball out of the air!

As the fans applauded the amazing catch, Liam slowed to a trot. Carter couldn't see his face beneath the cap, but he suspected his cousin's expression was grim. There was nothing he could do about that, though. Liam knew as well as he did that one of two things happened when a batter came to the plate: He got on base or made an out. There were countless factors that determined the outcome. This time, Charlie M.'s speed and agility had made the difference.

Carter struck out the next batter, Mason, in five pitches to end West's turn at bat.

"All right, boys, let's make the fifth inning the big one," Coach Harrison said when the players returned to the dugout. He bounced on his toes, his eyes snapping with excitement and energy. "Let's take the lead—and keep it! What do you say?"

"Yes!" the players shouted as one.

"Here's the order: Charlie S., Ash, Charlie M. Ready? Hands in the middle."

The boys circled up.

"Mid-Atlantic, one-two-three! Mid-Atlantic, one-two-three!"

Charlie S. grabbed a bat, stuck a helmet on his head, and hustled to the plate. He took a swing at the first pitch and smoked a grounder toward first. Mason got his glove on it and beat Charlie S. to the bag for out number one.

"You got this, Ash, you got this!" Carter cried.

Ash swung twice and missed twice. He fouled the third pitch directly at the first-base dugout. The boys inside instinctively ducked, even though they knew the fence would protect them. On the fourth pitch—

Ping!

"It's gone! It's gone! It's gone!" Carter screamed.

It wasn't a homer, though; the ball landed just out of

the center fielder's reach but was inside the fence. Ash ran from first to second and then second to third. He slid across the base just ahead of the cutoff man's throw.

"Hit 'em home, Charlie M.!" the Mid-Atlantic players shouted.

When Charlie M. fouled the ball three times, the shouts grew a little louder. The encouragement must have helped, though, because he lined the fourth pitch past the shortstop. He reached first—and Ash made it home!

West 6, Mid-Atlantic 5.

Allen hit into a double play, so that's where the score stayed. The board didn't change at the top of the sixth, either. Three West batters came up and faced Carter. All three returned to their dugout having failed to get on base.

"Bring it in, boys," Coach Harrison called. He gave them the shortest pep talk ever. "One run to tie. Two to win." He looked Carter in the eye and glanced at Charlie M. and Craig. "Some of us have been in this same position before. This time, I know we can leave the field with a different result. We can do this."

The players murmured their agreement. Then they said it louder. And finally, they shouted it at the top of their lungs. *We can do this!*

"Raj, you're up first. Then Ron and Carter."

Carter started. He'd forgotten that he'd taken Luke's place in the lineup and now followed Ron instead of Charlie M.

"Now pitching for West, Phillip DiMaggio."

And instead of facing Elton or Carmen, I'll be facing Phillip!

Ping!

The sound of bat meeting ball brought him back to the moment. Raj had singled. Ron took some big cuts but failed to connect.

I can do this, Carter thought as he walked to the batter's box. Suddenly, something Coach Harrison once said came back to him.

Just keep doing what you've been doing, and you'll walk off that field as winners—whether you win the game or not.

Carter nodded to himself and got into position. His green eyes met Phillip's piercing black ones. A frisson of electricity seemed to connect them.

"Go, Carter! Go, Carter! Go, Carter!" the Mid-Atlantic boys chanted. Carter blocked them out. Phillip wound up and threw. The pitch zipped through the air. Carter swung—and hit the ball. It wasn't a rocket like Liam's—Carter wasn't that kind of hitter, not yet, anyway—but it was good enough for a single and well-placed, too, bouncing into shallow right field. Raj put on a burst of speed and reached third.

Freddie was up next. Like Ron, he swung hard but missed three pitches to make out number two.

Now Stephen took his turn at bat. Carter's heart hammered in his chest. His legs tensed, ready to run if—

Ping!

Stephen got a hit! Carter raced to second. Raj motored home and scored!

Tie ball game! Carter wanted to dance a jig. But, of course, he didn't. He hid his excitement when, unbelievably, Phillip walked Charlie S. to load the bases. When Ash moved to the plate, though, he balled his hands into fists and lightly pounded them against his thighs.

Ash! Ash! Ash! his mind yelled.

Phillip wound up and threw. Ash uncoiled.

Pow!

Carter didn't wait to see where the ball went. Head down, he took off for home at a dead sprint.

"Gogogogogogogo!" the third-base coach yelled. Then, "Hit the dirt, Carter!"

He obeyed. The loose soil rolled beneath his buttocks as he slid feetfirst toward home.

Toward Liam, poised to make the catch and tag

him out. Toward victory, if he slid beneath the tag—or defeat, if he was a second too late.

Whap! The ball was in Liam's glove. His foot was inches from the plate. The glove swept down. His leg rode over the dish. There was an instant of complete silence, broken when the umpire made the call.

"Safe!"

Carter scored on the single! Mid-Atlantic won, 7 to 6!

If anyone had asked Carter the next day for a play-by-play of what had happened on the field next, he wouldn't have been able to tell them much. He'd been too caught up in the emotion of the moment to focus on the details.

What he did remember, very clearly, was seeing Liam as the players shook hands after the game. He broke away from the line and charged at his cousin. He grabbed him in a bear hug and held on tight. Liam returned the hug with equal ferocity. Someone took a video of that hug and posted it online. Within hours, it went viral.

What the video failed to record was their conversation:

"You better win tomorrow, dork," Liam said.

"I'll try, doofus," Carter replied.

Liam solemnly held up a finger. "As the great Jedi Master Yoda once said—"

"Do, or do not," Carter finished for him. "There is no try!"

"Yeah." Liam curled his finger so that he formed a fist. Carter lifted his fist, too. They brought them together, tapping once, twice, three times.

That's what Carter was thinking about the next afternoon as he stood on the mound of Howard J. Lamade Stadium for the final game of the Little League Baseball World Series. Although Carter didn't know exactly where Liam was in the stadium, he knew he was watching. So before he threw the first pitch, he raised his hand above his head and punched the air three times.

This one's for you, Liam!

CHAPTER
TWENTY-SEVEN

Late Sunday morning, Liam helped West win third place in the Little League Baseball World Series, defeating Japan 4–2. That afternoon, he sat on the Hill, surrounded by his teammates and their families to watch the tournament's title game between Mid-Atlantic and Australia. He added his voice to the cheers as the players were introduced. He quieted as the player pledge was recited, but in his head, he recited the familiar words, too.

I trust in God. I love my country and will respect its laws. I will play fair and strive to win, but win or lose, I will always do my best.

After the Parent and Volunteer pledge and pregame

warm-ups, Mid-Atlantic took the field while Australia prepared to bat. Carter, having thrown less than twenty pitches in the U.S. Championship the day before, was on the mound. Moments before the first pitch, Liam saw his cousin raise his fist and jab the air three times. He grinned.

"Right back at you, dork."

Up to that point in the tournament, Carter's pitching had been strong. In this game, it was downright amazing. He set down the first nine Australian batters in order, striking out seven with a combination of fluttering knuckleballs, blistering fastballs, and slow-moving changeups.

Mid-Atlantic, meanwhile, got a run on the board in the first when Ash knocked Craig home with an RBI double. They added another in the second inning when Charlie M. raced across the plate on Raj's single. The third inning saw Keith get his first hit, a single that advanced Ron to third. Ron and Keith reached home when Ash belted a double.

After three innings, the score read Australia 0, Mid-Atlantic 4.

Applause echoed through the stadium as Mid-Atlantic hustled onto the field for the top of the fourth.

"Hold 'em, Mid-Atlantic, you got this!" one loud fan cried out.

"Time to get on that board, mates!" a voice from a different section bellowed. If his cry wasn't enough of a clue, his accent left no doubt that he was rooting for Australia.

As if in response, Jon Burns blasted a fly ball that dropped out of Charlie S.'s reach in right field. As Charlie S. scrambled to pick it up, Jon dashed from first to second. Liam held his breath as Charlie S. whirled and threw to the cutoff man—then he groaned with disappointment when the throw was off target. By the time Mid-Atlantic recovered, Jon was safe at third.

Next up was Nigel, one of the other boys Carter and Liam had met in the pool. Nigel had just subbed into the game at first base, so Carter hadn't faced him before. On the Hill, Liam leaned forward, hands clenched.

"You got this, dork," he murmured.

Carter wound up and threw.

Ping!

Nigel's hit wasn't colossal, but it was well-placed, dropping into a hole behind Raj and in front of Charlie S. Jon sped home and Nigel reached first. The next batter popped out. The one after that struck out. When the inning's fifth hitter looked two pitches into Ash's glove for called strikes, Liam allowed himself to relax.

It looked like Nigel wouldn't advance any farther than first after all. Then—

Pow! The batter got all of Carter's third pitch! The ball rocketed far into the outfield and fell behind the fence for a two-run homer!

"Uh, oh. Liam, look at Carter."

Phillip's voice cut through the thunderous applause the home run had earned. Liam looked—and bit his lip. Carter was pounding the ball into his glove over and over. In the past, that gesture signaled anxiety.

"Think he's starting to freak out just a little?" Phillip asked.

Liam didn't answer. Instead, he watched his cousin intently. He was too far away to see Carter's face, but his posture spoke volumes. Liam smiled.

"He's not freaking out at all," he replied. "I think he's channeling his energy, focusing it so he can get the next batter out."

Sure enough, three pitches later, Carter had added another strikeout to his growing tally and brought the top of the inning to a close.

Mid-Atlantic 4, Australia 3. When Mid-Atlantic didn't add a run their turn at bat, that's what the scoreboard said at the end of the fourth inning, too. Carter and his teammates held off a scoring threat late in the fifth to keep their one-run lead, but they didn't widen the margin their turn at bat. Australia came up to bat in the top of the sixth with every chance in the world of tying the game and even taking the lead.

On the Hill, Liam tightened his hands into fists and began to pound them on his thighs. "Carter. Carter. Carter." He kept his chant very low; yelling it would have been unsportsmanlike.

Carter leaned in and took the signal. He wound up, reared back, and threw. The batter swung. Missed.

"Strike one!"

The batter nicked the next pitch, but the ball danced outside the first-base line for strike two. He fanned the third for strike three.

"Two more to go, dork. You got this," Liam mumbled.

But the next batter got a single. And the third clipped a pitch and sent it bouncing toward shortstop.

Now Liam did raise his voice. "Go, Raj! Go!" he screamed.

Raj scooped up the ball and sent it to Freddie at second.

"Out!" the umpire cried, jerking a thumb over his shoulder.

The batter sprinted full tilt. Freddie threw to Keith

at first. The ball hit Keith's outstretched glove. The batter's foot touched the base. But which happened first?

A hush fell over the stadium as thousands of spectators waited for the call. Liam's heart drubbed once. Then—

"Out!"

Final score: Mid-Atlantic 4, Australia 3.

Liam wished he could swarm the field and join the celebration. He would have given a lot to circle the bases with Carter in the traditional World Series victory lap. But he settled for jumping up and down and bellowing at the top of his lungs.

CHAPTER
TWENTY-EIGHT

Hey, dork, you come down off cloud nine yet?"

Carter turned to see Liam hurrying across the rec room toward him. He grinned. "Not yet, but maybe on the ride home I will!"

It was Monday morning. The teams still in Williamsport were packing up and preparing to depart for home. As wonderful an experience as the World Series had been, Carter had to admit he was looking forward to sleeping in his own bed that night. After all, it had been nearly a month since he'd done so!

Still, he wouldn't have traded his summer for any other. Winning the World Series had been magical, a dream come true. The hours after the World Series win had been an absolute whirlwind of congratulations from family and friends, interviews with the press, and celebrations with his teammates. But for Carter, the win had been the icing on the cake that was playing baseball.

Once the postgame craziness died down, Carter asked his team host if he could see Jon Burns. He wanted to be sure to offer his compliments to the boy and his teammates before they left the country.

"I'm not gonna lie to you, Carter," Jon said when they met. "I wanted to win something fierce. But I'm glad we lost to you."

"Really? Why?"

Jon laughed. "Because Mid-Atlantic is a great team. And even better, you're great guys; well, the ones I've met, anyway."

Carter flushed, pleased but a little embarrassed, too. "Thanks, man."

"To be honest, I was a bit gobsmacked to even be here," Jon added. "This has been the most incredible journey ever. I'm not talking just about playing ball. Meeting so many people from so many different countries...it's changed the way I look at the world, you know? Now when I hear about stuff happening in Mexico, or Canada, or the Netherlands, or anywhere in the

U.S., I'll have faces to put with the places. It makes the countries more real somehow."

Carter nodded. He knew just what Jon meant and agreed with him one hundred percent.

Jon grinned with pride. "World travelers and top of the Internationals! Are we going home with the World Series title? No. Are we going home winners? Too right we are!"

Then he invited Carter to find him online so they could stay in touch. "And if you ever come Down Under, you've got a place to stay!"

Carter extended the same invitations to Jon. As he watched the big blond boy saunter off, he wondered if he would ever see him again in person.

Now it was Monday morning, and Carter had been wondering if he'd see Liam before he left Williamsport. That's when Liam had called his name.

"When do you guys take off?" he asked.

"The bus leaves pretty soon," Carter replied. "So I guess this is good—"

"Carter!" A shout from Phillip interrupted them. Phillip came running up. Panting, he thrust a bag at Carter and said, "This is for you."

"What is it?"

Phillip rolled his eyes. "Duh, look inside and find out."

Carter pulled out a T-shirt and held it up by its edges. His eyes widened. "It's from this year's baseball camp."

"How'd you get that?" Liam asked.

"Mr. Matthews helped me find one," Phillip replied. He tapped the shirt's shoulder. "There's an inscription."

Scrawled on the cloth was a handwritten message. Carter read it out loud. *"To Carter, who can throw a great knuckleball, from Phillip, who can be a real knucklehead."*

Carter didn't say anything else for a long moment. Then he started chuckling. His chuckle turned into a full laugh.

"Thanks, man," he managed to say. He flung the shirt over his shoulder and put out his hand.

Phillip shook it. "Oh, and just one more thing," he said with a grin. "Congratulations on winning the World Series."

"Thanks," Carter said again. "I wish we could have all won but—"

Phillip cut him off. "Dude, it's okay. I won last year, remember? Besides, my World Series was made the minute I met Nathan Daly! Not that I would have minded another victory, but—man, how awesome was that night at the restaurant? And how about just being in Williamsport in the first place?" He left then with a last backward wave and a smile.

Carter turned back to Liam. His smile faded. "So," he said, stabbing his toe at the ground.

"So. Guess I'll see you around," Liam replied.

"Not if I see you first."

"Dork."

"Doofus."

The boys hugged tightly. Then Liam left, too.

Five hours later, Carter stepped through the front door of his house and gave a huge sigh. His mother came up from behind and brushed her fingers lightly over his head. "You okay?"

"Yeah," he said. "Just happy to be home."

Mr. Jones took his suitcase from him. "Head on upstairs. I'll take care of this."

"And I'll bring you something to eat. But first, I think I see someone coming who missed you a whole lot!"

Carter looked over his shoulder and grinned. Coming up the walkway was Rachel Warburton. Lucky Boy was at her side. When the dog saw Carter, he pulled free and raced the rest of the way to the house. Carter knelt and buried his face in the warm fur.

"Welcome home," Rachel said warmly.

"Thanks. You want to come in?"

"Can't. But I'll see you soon."

Carter did see Rachel soon—and tons of other people from Forest Park, too, at a town-wide celebration at the Diamond Champs the next afternoon. Mrs. LaBrie had organized the whole thing, from balloons to refreshments to a temporary stage for the players and coaches to use for speeches.

"Did you know about this?" Carter asked Ash as they made their way through the crowd to join their teammates on the stage.

"No," Ash said. "It was a total surprise!"

Something occurred to Carter. "Hey," he said excitedly. "Maybe *this* is the surprise your mom was talking about! Maybe you aren't moving after all!"

Ash didn't look convinced, but he didn't have time to argue as his mother had taken the microphone and was beckoning him to come forward.

"As most of you know," Mrs. LaBrie said to the crowd gathered in front of them, "Ash and I moved here less than a year ago. We've been very happy here and are so pleased that this facility"—she indicated the Diamond Champs—"has become a favorite of so many. That being said, it has been a challenge running it single-handedly. So it's time for a change."

Ash threw a wretched look at Carter. *Here it comes,* his look seemed to say.

Suddenly, there was a murmur at the back of the crowd. The people parted. A tall blond man strode toward the stage. Even before Carter heard Ash gasp, he realized who it was.

"Dad!" Ash hurled himself off the stage and into his father's arms.

"Ladies and gentlemen, in case you haven't figured it out, that man is my husband, Andrew LaBrie. You'll be seeing a lot of him from now on because he's come home to stay."

Ash's jaw dropped. "You have? We're—we're not moving? But what about your job with the military?"

Mr. LaBrie laughed. "I'll explain all that later. But to answer your question: I'm the only one moving, and the only place I'm moving to is right here."

Carter had been overjoyed when Mid-Atlantic won the World Series. But he was pretty sure the happiness he saw on Ash's face at that moment was almost greater. Almost.

CHAPTER
TWENTY-NINE

Liam opened his eyes and stared at the ceiling. It was the first time in a long time he'd looked at that particular patch. If he looked closely enough, he could see the faint mark he'd left there more than a year ago when he'd been hurling a small pink rubber ball at the spot.

It was Christmas morning. He was in the top bunk in Carter's bedroom. Below, he could hear Carter breathing deeply, so he knew his cousin was still fast asleep. He laced his fingers beneath his head and thought about everything that had happened since he'd last slept in this bed: moving to California, meeting Sean and Rodney, making things right with Phillip, going to the World Series...

Carter's door creaked open. Liam looked over to

see a small black-and-tan dog nose its way inside. He grinned. "Hey there, Lucky Boy," he whispered. Lucky Boy trotted to the bed, tail wagging madly, and began licking Carter's face.

"Eeesh! Cut it out, cut it out!" Carter rasped, his voice thick with sleep.

"Shhh," Liam warned. "You'll wake me up!"

Carter chuckled. "Merry Christmas, doofus!"

"Merry Christmas, dork!"

Twenty minutes later, they'd roused the rest of the household. Now everyone was gathered in the Joneses' living room by the tree, opening presents. Liam and Carter had two special cards waiting for them. One was from Jon Burns, the boy from Australia.

"Merry Christmas from Oz!" Jon's message read. "Don't spend this all in one place! Ha-ha!"

Inside the card were two identical coins. On one side was a profile of the queen of England, Elizabeth II. On the other was the image of a swimming platypus with 20 stamped over it, indicating the silver coin was worth twenty Australian cents.

"Cool!" Liam and Carter exclaimed together.

"Did you send him something?" Melanie asked.

"We mailed him two state quarters," Carter replied.

"California and Pennsylvania. We sent the same thing to Kita Hiro in Japan, too. It was Liam's idea."

"Nice!" Melanie nodded approvingly.

The boys opened the card from Kita next. Two more coins dropped out. Liam gave one to Carter and examined the other.

The coin was a fifty yen piece. It had chrysanthemum flowers on one side and Japanese symbols and numbers on the other. But the most interesting thing was the single hole punched out of the center.

"Kita says the flower is an important symbol in Japan," Carter said, reading the letter, "and that the hole is to help vision-impaired people identify the coin."

Everyone admired the international coins and cards, then returned to their own gifts.

Liam had just unwrapped a new book by his favorite sports author when his mother handed him a small package. She handed an identical one to Melanie.

"Open them together," she requested. She down next to her husband and leaned against him, smiling.

Liam pulled off the bow, tore the paper, and lifted the lid from a small white box. Inside was a key. He held it up and looked at his parents, puzzled. Melanie looked equally confused.

"I know this isn't a car key," she said. "So what does it go to?"

Mr. McGrath pointed out the side window of the living room. "That."

Liam stared out the window. "All I see is Mrs. Webber's house," he said.

"That's right," Mrs. McGrath said. "Only it's not Mrs. Webber's anymore."

Liam's heart skipped a beat. He looked at the key in his hand and then back to the house. "So who owns it now?"

His parents smiled. "We do," his mother replied. "Or we will," she amended, "at the end of June."

"I don't understand," Melanie said, her brow furrowed.

"I do!" Liam shouted. "We're moving back here, aren't we?"

Melanie's eyes widened. "Is that true?"

Mrs. McGrath nodded happily. "Right after the school year," she said. "Turns out there's a big demand for eco-friendly playground equipment on the East Coast. My company decided to open a branch here. They asked me to run it. I said yes."

Liam barely heard the explanation. He was too busy absorbing the fact that—

"You're moving back!" Carter tackled him, laughing joyfully.

"Now that's what I call a Christmas present!" Liam cried as he tumbled to the floor. Then he glanced at Melanie. She had been thrilled to move to California. "Hey, you're okay with this, aren't you?"

Melanie smiled broadly. "Are you kidding? Of course I am!" She turned to her parents. "Now if I get into the film school in New York City, you guys will be right here instead of across the country!"

"Film school? I thought you wanted to be an actor!" Liam asked. He knew his sister, who was going to be a senior in high school, had been looking at a lot of colleges, but he hadn't really paid attention to which ones she was interested in.

"I like acting," she said, "but turns out I like being behind the camera even more. I found that out this summer while I was making my Little League film. Speaking of which…" She got up and put a gift bag in Liam's hands. "Here's your copy."

Liam peeked at the DVD inside the bag. "We'll watch this later, after presents, okay?"

And that's what they did. Liam loved every minute of it and told his sister so. She blushed at the compliment but couldn't stop smiling.

Later in the day, Rachel and a few boys came over to see Liam. After making fun of his longer hair—"Dude, what happened to your crew cut? You look all California!"—and eating Christmas cookies, they trooped down to the basement for some Ping-Pong.

That evening, Liam and Carter video-chatted in Carter's bedroom with Rodney and Sean. True friends that they were, they told Liam how happy they were for him about the move. "At least we'll get one more season of baseball with you, and this year it'll be Junior Division!" Rodney pointed out. "But what'll you do if you're named to the Ravenna All-Stars again?"

"Guess I'll just give my spot to Sean," Liam joked.

Sean puffed out his chest. "Thanks, but no thanks. I'm planning to earn one for myself."

They ended the chat session soon after that and went downstairs. Carter grabbed Lucky Boy's leash and held it up for Liam to see. "Feel like taking a walk?"

"As long as you don't clip that to my collar," Liam said, "sure."

Carter told their parents what they were doing, found a flashlight, and called for Lucky Boy. By unspoken agreement, they headed for the path in the woods behind Carter's house. Ten minutes later, they reached the hideout.

"Looks pretty much the same," Liam said. "Think the box is still there?"

Carter crawled inside and dragged out a dark green plastic box. "Yep." Inside the box were old beach towels and two more flashlights. They spread out the towels and lay down. Nose to the ground, Lucky Boy went in search of smells.

Liam rested his head on his hands and stared up through a gap in the trees to a patch of stars. His breath came out in frosty puffs. "Hey, dork," he said after a long silence.

"Yeah, doofus?"

"I'm moving back this summer." He sat up. "You know, we've still got a lot of Little League seasons ahead of us. There's Fall Ball next September, and then it's onto the Intermediate Division. After that, Junior Division. From there, we'll go to the Senior League and then the Big League. We'll both get on the All-Star teams and reach the World Series for all of them. No, not just reach them—win them!"

Carter laughed. "One step at a time, doofus!"

"Dork," Liam replied, grinning broadly. "With you and me teamed up again, we're going to go all the way!"

"And don't forget Ash, and Charlie M., and—" Carter started to add.

"Yeah, yeah, everyone and anyone who's a player! We'd be unstoppable!"

He lay back down and held up a fist. Carter did the same. And lying together beneath the Christmas night sky, they fist-bumped three times.

WHAT IS LITTLE LEAGUE®?

With nearly 165,000 teams in all 50 states and over 80 other countries across the globe, Little League® Baseball and Softball is the world's largest organized youth sports program! Many of today's Major League players started their baseball careers in Little League Baseball, including Derek Jeter, David Wright, Justin Verlander, and Adrian Gonzalez.

Little League® is a nonprofit organization that works to teach the principles of sportsmanship, fair play, and teamwork. Concentrating on discipline, character, and courage, Little League is focused on more than just developing athletes: It helps to create upstanding citizens.

Carl Stotz established Little League in 1939 in Williamsport, Pennsylvania. The first league only had three teams and played six innings, but by 1946, there were already twelve leagues throughout the state of Pennsylvania. The following year, 1947, was the first year that the Little League Baseball® World Series was played, and it has continued to be played every August since then.

In 1951, Little League Baseball expanded internationally, and the first permanent leagues to form outside of the United States were on either end of the Panama Canal. Little League Baseball later moved to nearby South Williamsport, Pennsylvania, and a second stadium, the Little League Volunteer Stadium, was opened in 2001.

Some key moments in Little League history:

- **1957** The Monterrey, Mexico, team became the first international team to win the World Series.
- **1964** Little League was granted a federal charter.
- **1974** The federal charter was amended to allow girls to join Little League.
- **1982** The Peter J. McGovern Little League Museum opened.
- **1989** Little League introduced the Challenger Division.
- **2001** The World Series expanded from eight to sixteen teams to provide a greater opportunity for children to participate in the World Series.
- **2014** Little League celebrates its 75th anniversary.

HOW DOES A LITTLE LEAGUE®
TEAM GET TO THE WORLD SERIES?

In order to play in the Little League Baseball® World Series, a player must first be a part of a regular-season Little League, and then be selected as part of the league's All-Star team, consisting of players ages 11 to 13 from any of the teams. The All-Star teams compete in district, sectional, and state tournaments to become their state champions. The state champions then compete to represent one of eight different geographic regions of the United States (New England, Mid-Atlantic, Southeast, Great Lakes, Midwest, Northwest, Southwest, and West). All eight of the Regional Tournament winners play in the Little League Baseball World Series.

The eight International Tournament winners (representing Asia-Pacific and Middle East, Australia, Canada, the Caribbean, Europe and Africa, Mexico, Japan, and Latin America) also come to the Little League Baseball World Series in Williamsport, Pennsylvania.

The eight U.S. Regional Tournament winners compete in the United States Bracket of the Little League

Baseball World Series, and the International Tournament winners compete in the International Bracket.

Over eleven days, the Little League Baseball World Series proceeds until a winning U.S. Championship team and International Championship team are determined. The final World Series Championship Game is played between the U.S. Champions and the International Champions.

WANT TO LEARN MORE?

Visit the *World of Little League, Peter J. McGovern Museum, and Official Store* in South Williamsport, Pennsylvania! When you visit, you'll find pictures, interactive displays, films, and exhibits showing the history and innovations of Little League.

More information is available at
LittleLeagueMuseum.org

HOW CAN I JOIN A
LITTLE LEAGUE® TEAM?

If you have access to the Internet, you can see if your community has a local league by going to LittleLeague.org and clicking on "Find a League." You can also visit one of our regional offices:

US REGIONAL OFFICES:

Western Region Headquarters (AK, AZ, CA, HI, ID, MT, NV, OR, UT, WA, and WY)
6707 Little League Drive
San Bernardino, CA 92407
E-MAIL: westregion@LittleLeague.org

Southwestern Region Headquarters (AR, CO, LA, MS, NM, OK, and TX)
3700 South University Parks Drive
Waco, TX 76706
E-MAIL: southwestregion@LittleLeague.org

Central Region Headquarters (IA, IL, IN, KS, KY, MI, MN, MO, ND, NE, OH, SD, and WI)
9802 E. Little League Drive
Indianapolis, IN 46235
E-MAIL: centralregion@LittleLeague.org

Southeastern Region Headquarters (AL, FL, GA, NC, SC, TN, VA, and WV)
PO Box 7557
Warner Robins, GA 31095
E-MAIL: southeastregion@LittleLeague.org

Eastern Region Headquarters (CT, DC, DE, MA, MD, ME, NH, NJ, NY, PA, RI, and VT)
PO Box 2926
Bristol, CT 06011
E-MAIL: eastregion@LittleLeague.org

INTERNATIONAL REGIONAL OFFICES:
CANADIAN REGION (serving all of Canada)
Canadian Little League Headquarters
235 Dale Avenue
Ottawa, ONT
Canada K1G OH6
E-MAIL: Canada@LittleLeague.org

ASIA-PACIFIC REGION (serving all of Asia and Australia)
Asia-Pacific Regional Director
C/O Hong Kong Little League
Room 1005, Sports House
1 Stadium Path
Causeway Bay, Hong Kong
E-MAIL: bhc368@netvigator.com

EUROPE, MIDDLE EAST & AFRICA REGION
(serving all of Europe, the Middle East, and Africa)
Little League Europe
Al. Meleg Legi 1
Kutno, 99-300, Poland
E-MAIL: Europe@LittleLeague.org

LATIN AMERICA REGION (serving Mexico and Latin American regions)
Latin America Little League Headquarters
PO Box 10237
Caparra Heights, Puerto Rico 00922-0237
E-MAIL: LatinAmerica@LittleLeague.org

Fill in the blanks with the words below to solve the twelve-letter mystery phrase!

Hints: Match the number of blanks to the number of letters in each word. Be sure the words make sense both horizontally and vertically!

Three Letters:
ACE
BAT
CAP
NAB

Four Letters:
GAME
SAFE

Five Letters:
CATCH
COACH
FIRST
GLOVE
HOMER
PITCH
SLIDE
THROW

Six Letters:
RUNNER
STRIKE

Eight Letters:
BASE HITS
BASEBALL
CHAMPION

B	A	S	E	B	A	L	L		B			
A		A				I		A		C		
T		F	I	R	S	T		S		H		T
		E		U		T		E		A		H
				N		L		H	O	M	E	R
		P		N		E		I		P		O
S	L	I	D	E		L		T		I		W
T		T		R		E		S		O		
R		C			A		C		N	A	B	
I		H		G	L	O	V	E				
K			C	U		A		A				
E		G	A	M	E		C	A	T	C	H	
		P		H			E					

204